David Starr Jordan

The story of the innumerable company, and other sketches

David Starr Jordan

The story of the innumerable company, and other sketches

ISBN/EAN: 9783743328808

Manufactured in Europe, USA, Canada, Australia, Japa

Cover: Foto ©ninafisch / pixelio.de

Manufactured and distributed by brebook publishing software
(www.brebook.com)

David Starr Jordan

The story of the innumerable company, and other sketches

THE STORY OF THE INNUMERABLE COMPANY, AND OTHER SKETCHES

BY

DAVID STARR JORDAN

PRESIDENT OF LELAND STANFORD JUNIOR UNIVERSITY

SAN FRANCISCO

THE WHITAKER & RAY COMPANY

INCORPORATED)

1896

PREFATORY NOTE.

THIS volume is made up of separate sketches, historical or allegorical, having in some degree a bond of union in the idea of "the higher sacrifice."

I am under obligations to Professor William R. Dudley for the use of a photograph of a record of Father Serra. This was secured through the kindness of the late Father Casanova, of Monterey.

PALO ALTO, CAL., June 1, 1896.

CONTENTS.

ILLUSTRATIONS.

Men told me, Lord, it was a vale of tears
Where Thou hast placed me, wickedness and woe
My twain companions whereso I might go;
That I through ten and threescore weary years
Should stumble on beset by pains and fears,
Fierce conflict round me, passions hot within,
Enjoyment brief and fatal but in sin.
When all was ended then should I demand
Full compensation from thine austere hand;
For, 'tis thy pleasure, all temptation past,
To be not just but generous at last.

Lord, here am I, my threescore years and ten
All counted to the full; I've fought thy fight,
Crossed thy dark valleys, scaled thy rocks' harsh height,
Borne all the burdens Thou dost lay on men
With hand unsparing threescore years and ten.
Before Thee now I make my claim, O Lord,—
What shall I pray Thee as a meet reward?

I ask for nothing. Let the balance fall!
All that I am or know or may confess
But swells the weight of mine indebtedness;
Burdens and sorrows stand transfigured all;
Thy hand's rude buffet turns to a caress,
For Love, with all the rest, Thou gavest me here,
And Love is Heaven's very atmosphere.
Lo, I have dwelt with Thee, Lord. Let me die.
I could no more through all eternity.

THE STORY OF THE INNUMERABLE
COMPANY.

THERE was once a great mountain which rose
from the shore of the sea, and on its flanks it
bore a mighty forest. Beyond the crest of the
mountain were ridges and valleys, peaks and
chasms, springs and torrents. Farther on lay
a sandy desert, which stretched its monotonous
breadth to the shore of a wide, swift river. What
lay beyond the river no one knew, because its
shores were always hid in azure mist.

Year by year there came up from the shore of
the sea an Innumerable Company. Each one must
cross the mountain and the forest, faring onward
toward the desert and the river. And this was one
condition of the journey — that whosoever came to
the river must breast its waters alone. Why this
was so, no one could tell; nor did any one know
aught of the land beyond. For of the multitude
who had crossed the river not one had ever returned.

As time went on there came to be paths through

the forest. Those who went first left traces to serve
as guides for those coming after. Some put marks
on the trees; some built little cairns of stones to
show the way they had taken in going around great
rocks. Those who followed found these marks and
added to them. And many of the travelers left
little charts which showed where the cliffs and
chasms were and by what means one could reach
the hidden springs. So in time it came to pass
that there was scarcely a tree on the mountain
which bore not some traveler's mark; there was
scarcely a rock that had not a cairn of stones
upon it.

In early times there was One who came up from
the sea and made the journey over the mountain
and across the desert by a way so fair that the
memory of it became a part of the story of the
forest. Men spoke to each other of his way, and
many wished to find it out, that haply they might
walk therein. He, too, had left a Chart, which those
who followed him had carefully kept, and from
which they had drawn help in many times of need.

The way he went was not the shortest way, nor
was it the easiest. The ways that are short and
easy lead not over the mountain. But his was the
most *repaying* way. It led by the noblest trees, the

fairest outlooks, the sweetest springs, the greenest
pastures, and the shadow of great rocks in the
desert. And the chart of his way which he left
was very simple and very plain — easy to understand. Even a child might use it. And, indeed,
there were many children who did so.

On this chart were the chief landmarks of the
region — the mountain with its forest, the desert
with its green oases, the paths to the hidden springs.
But there were not many details. The old cairns
were not marked upon it, and when two paths led
alike over the mountain, there was no sign to show
that one was to be taken rather than the other.
Not much was said as to what food one should
take, or what raiment one should wear, or by what
means one should defend himself. But there were
many simple directions as to how one should act
on the road, and by what signs he should know
the right path. One ought to look upward, and
not downward; to look forward, and not backward;
to be always ready to give a helping hand to his
neighbor: and whomsoever one meets is one's
neighbor, he said.

As to the desert, one need not dread it; nor
should one fear the river, for the lands beyond it
were sweet and fair. Moreover, one should learn

to know the forest, that he might choose his course wisely. And this knowledge each one should seek for himself. For, as he said, " If the blind lead the blind, both shall fall into the ditch."

There were many who followed his way and gave heed to his precepts. The path seemed dangerous at times, especially at the outset; for it lay along dizzy heights, through tangled underwood, and across swollen torrents. But after a while all these were left behind. The way passed on between cleft rocks, into green pastures, and by still waters; and in the desert were sweet springs which gave forth abundantly.

But some who tried to follow him said that his Chart was not explicit enough. Every step in the journey, they contended, should be laid out exactly; for to travel safely one should never be left in doubt.

Now, it chanced that on the slope of the mountain there was a huge granite rock, which stood in the midst of the way. Some of the travelers passed to the right of it, while others turned to the left. Strangely enough, the Chart said nothing concerning this rock. No hint was given as to how one should pass by it.

When they came to the rock, many of the travelers took counsel one of another, and at last a great multitude was gathered there. Which way had he taken? For in the path he took they must surely go. Many scanned the rock on every side, to find if haply he had left some secret mark upon it. But they found none; or, rather, no one could convince the others that the hidden marks he found were intended for their guidance.

At nightfall, after much discussion, the old men in the council gave their decision. The safe way led to the right. So he who kept the Chart marked upon it the place of the rock, and he wrote upon the Chart that the one true path leads to the right. Henceforth each man should know the way he must go.

Moreover, those who bore the records showed that this decision was justified. They wrote upon the Chart a long argument, chain upon chain and reason upon reason, to prove that from the beginning it was decreed that by this rock should the destiny of man be tested.

But in spite of argument, there were still some who chose the left-hand path because they verily believed that this was the only right way. They, too, justified their course by arguments, line upon line and precept upon precept. And each band tried to make its following as large as it could.

Some men stood all day by the side of the rock, urging people to come with them to the right or to the left. For, strangely enough, although each man had his own journey to make, and must cross the river at last alone, he was eager that all others should go along with him.

And as each band grew larger, its members took pride in the growth of its numbers. In the larger bands, trumpets were blown, harps were sounded, and banners were waved in the wind. Those who walked shoulder to shoulder under waving flags to the sound of trumpets felt secure and confident, while those who journeyed alone seemed always to walk with fear and trembling. It was said in the old Chart that where two or three were gathered together on the way, strength and courage would be given them. But men could not believe this, and few had the heart to test whether it were true or no.

So the bands went on to the right or to the left, each in its chosen path. But after they had passed the first great rock, they came to other rocks and trees and places of doubt. Other councils were held, and at each step there were some who would not abide by the decision of the elders. So these from time to time went their own ways. And they made new inscriptions on the Chart, and erased the old ones, each according to his own ideas. And there was much pushing and jostling when the bands separated themselves one from another.

At last one of the oldest travelers in the largest band — a man with a long white beard, and wise with the experience of years — arose and said that not in anger, nor in strife, should they journey on. Discord and contention arise from difference of opinion. Let all men but think alike, and they will walk in peace and harmony. Let each band choose a leader. Let him carry the Chart, and let him night and day pore over its precepts. No one else need distress himself. One had only to keep step on the road, and to follow whithersoever the leader might direct.

So the people chose a leader — a man grave and serious, wise in the lore of the forest and the desert. He noted on the Chart each rock and tree, drawing in sharp outlines every detail in the only safe path. Moreover, all deviating trails he marked with the symbol of danger.

And it came to pass that day by day other bands followed, and to them the Chart was given as he had left it. And these bands, too, chose leaders, whose part it was to interpret the Chart. But each one of these added to the Chart some better way of his own, some short cut he had found, or some new trail not marked with the proper sign of warning.

And with all these changes and additions, as time went on, the true way became very hard to find. At one point, so the story is told, there were twenty-nine distinct paths, leading in as many directions; each of these, if the Chart be true, came to its end in some frightful chasm. With these there was a single narrow trail that led to safety; but no two leaders could agree as to which was the right trail. One thing only was certain: the true way was very hard to find, and no traveler might discover it unaided.

And some declared that the Chart was complicated beyond all need. There was one who said, "The multiplication of non-essentials has become the bane of the forest." Even a little meadow which he had found, and which he called the "Saints' Rest," was so entangled in paths and counterpaths that once out of sight of it one could never find it again.

All this time there were many bands that wandered about in circles, finding everywhere cairns of stones, but no way of escape. Still others remained day after day in the shadow of great rocks, disputing and doubting as to how they should pass by them. There were arguments and precedents enough for any course; but arguments and precedents made no man sure.

And it came to pass that most travelers followed the band they found nearest. At last, to join some band became their only care. And they looked with pity and distrust upon those who traveled alone.

But the bands all made their way very slowly. No matter how wise the leader, not all were ready to move at once, and not all could keep step to the sound of even the slowest trumpet. There was often much ado at nightfall over the pitching of the tents, and many were crowded out into the forest. At times also, in the presence of danger, fear spread through the band, and many of the weaker ones were trampled on and sorely hurt.

Then, too, as they passed through the rocky defiles, some of them lost sight of the banners, and then the others would wait for them, or perchance leave them behind, to struggle on as best they might without chart or guide.

And there were those who spoke in this wise: "Many paths lead over the mountain, and sooner or later all come to the desert and the river. It does not matter where we walk; the question is, How? We cannot know step by step the way he went. Let us walk by faith, as he walked. If our spirit is like his, we shall not lack for guidance when we come to the crossing of the ways." And so they fared on. But many doubted their own promptings. "Tell me, am I right?" each one asked of his neighbor; and his neighbor asked it again of him. And those who were in doubt followed those who were sure.

So it came to pass that these who walked by faith likewise gathered themselves into great companies, and each company followed some leader. Some of these leaders had the gift of woodcraft, and saw clearly into the very nature of things. But some were only headstrong, and these proved to be but blind leaders of the blind.

Then one said, "We must not be filled with our own conceit, but must humbly imitate him. We must try to work as he worked; to rest as he rested; to sleep as he slept. The deeds we do should be those he did, and those only. For on his Chart he has told us, not the way he went past rocks and trees, but the actions with which his days were filled." Then those who tried to do as he had done, moved by his motives and acting through his deeds, found the way wonderfully easy. The days and the hours seemed all too short for the joy with which they were filled.

But, again, there were many who said that his directions were not explicit enough. The Chart said so little. "That we may make no mistake," they said, " we must gather ourselves in bands and choose leaders. We cannot act as he acted unless there is some one to show us how."

Thus it came to pass that leaders were chosen who could do everything that he had done, in all respects, according to his method. And they added to the Chart the record of their own practices — not only that "He did thus and so," but also, "Thus and so he did *not* do." "Thus and thus did he eat bread, and thus only. Thus and thus did he loose his sandals. In this way only gave he bread and wine. Here on the way he fasted; there he feasted. At this turn of the road he looked upward thus, shading his eyes with his hand. Here he anointed his feet; there his face wore a sad smile. Such was the cut of his coat; of this wood was his staff; of such a number of words his prayer." And many were comforted in the thought that for every turn in the road there was some definite thing which he had done, and which they, too, might perform.

Thus the duties of every moment were fixed. But as the days went on these duties grew more and more difficult. No one had time to look at the rocks or trees; no one could cast his eyes over a noble prospect; no one could stop to rest by the sweet fountains or in the refreshing shadows. One could hardly give a moment to such things, lest he should overlook some needful service.

Then many lost heart, and said that surely he cared not for times and observances, else he would have said more about them. When he made the journey, it was his chief reproach that he heeded not these things. With him, ceremony or observance rose directly out of the need for it, each one as the need was felt. To imitate him is to feel as he felt. With him feelings gave rise to word and action. "So will it be with us. It is not for us to imitate him in the fashion of his coat or the cut of his beard. He went over the road giving help and comfort, as the sun gives light or the flowers shed fragrance, all unconscious of the good he did." And in this wise did many imitate him. They turned aside the boughs of the trees, that the sunshine of heaven might fall upon their neighbors. And behold, the same sunshine fell upon them also. They removed the stones from the road, that others might not stumble over them. And others removed the stones from their way also.

But many were still in doubt and hesitation. The record, they said, was not explicit enough. They counseled together, and gathered in bands, and chose leaders who should tell them how to feel. And the leaders gave close heed to all his feelings and to the times and seasons proper to each. Here he was joyous, and at a signal all the band broke into merry laughter. Here he was stern, and the multitude set its teeth. There he wept, and tears fell like rain from innumerable eyes.

As time went on, repeated action made action easy. The springs of feeling were readily troubled. Still each one felt, or tried to feel, all that he should have felt. No one dared admit to his fellows that his tears were a sham, his joy a pretense, his sadness a lie. But often, in the bottom of their hearts, men would confess with real tears that they had no genuine feeling there.

Then the people asked for leaders who could bring out real feelings. And there arose leaders, who, by terrible words, could fill the hearts with fear; by burning words, could stir the embers of zeal; by the

intensity of their own passions, could fill the throng
with pity, with sorrow, or with indignation. And
the multitude hung on their lips; for they sought
for feelings real and not simulated.

But here again division arose; for not all were
touched alike by those who had power over the
hearts of men. Some followed the leader who
moved them to tears; others chose him who filled
them with fear and trembling. Still others loved
to linger in the dark shadow of remorse. Some
said that right emotions were roused by loud and
ringing tones. Some said that the tones should be
sad and sweet.

Then there were some who said that feelings such
as all these were idle and common. When he trod
the way of old, it was with radiant eyes and with
uplifted heart. He saw through the veil of clouds to
the glory which lay beyond. We follow him best
when we too are uplifted. Now and then on the
way come to us moments of exultation, when we
tread in his very footsteps. These are the precious
moments; then our way is his way. In the rosy
mists of morning, we may behold the glory which
encompassed him. In moments of silent commun-
ion in the forest, we may feel his peace steal over us.
In the gentle rain that falls upon the just and the

unjust, we may know the soft pity of his tears. When the sun declines, its last rays touch with gold the far-off mountain tops beyond the great river.

And the uplifting of great moments, filling the souls of men with peace that passeth understanding, came to many. As they went their way, this peace fell upon their neighbors also. And no man did aught to make them afraid. And others sought to go with these, and thus they became a great band.

So they chose as their leaders those whose visions were brightest. And they made for themselves a banner like the white mist flung out from the mountain-tops at the rising of the sun. They spoke much to each other concerning the white banner and the peace which filled their souls.

But as they journeyed along, the dust of the way dimmed the banner, and the bright visions one by one faded away. At last they came no more.

Then the people murmured and called upon the leaders to grant them some brighter vision, something that all could see and feel at once — some sign by which they might know that they were still in his way. "Cause that a path be opened through the thicket," they said, " and let a white dove come forth to lead us on; or, let the mists beyond the river part for a moment, that we may behold the far country beyond."

And one of the leaders standing at the head of the column, clothed in the morning light as with a garment, raised his staff high in the air. The sun's rays fell upon it, touching the morning mists with gold, and threw across them the long shadow of the upraised staff. The shadow fell far out across the plains, and about it was a halo of bright light. And all the band looked joyfully at the vision. Adown the slope of the mountain and out into the plain they followed the way of the shadow. And all the time the white banner waved at the head of the column. The people said little to one another, but that little was a word of praise and rejoicing.

But it came to pass, as the day wore on, that the sun rose in the sky, and drew the mists up from the valley. With them vanished the long shadow of the staff, and in its place appeared the sandy plain. The feet of the people were sore with the rocks and stones. The air was thick with dust. Their hearts were uplifted no longer. Instead they were filled with doubt and distress.

And the people repined and murmured against their leader. But the leader said that all was well; even in the way he went there had been stones and hindrances. More than once had he carried a heavy burden along a dusty road. But he never doubted nor complained, and so the radiance round about him never faded away.

But all the more the people clamored for a sign. Let the bright vision of the morning appear to us again. At length, worn with much entreaty, the leader raised once more his staff above his head. The sun at noon fell upon it. But as the people gazed they saw no long line of radiance stretching out across the plains amid a halo of shining mist. The shadow of the staff was a little shapeless mark upon the sand at their very feet.

Then the leader cast his staff away and went by himself alone, sad and sorrowful. That night, as he lay by the roadside, he looked upward to the clear, calm, honest stars. They seemed to say to him, "See all things as they really are. This was his way. 'In spirit and in truth' means in the light of no illusion. Not all the visions of mist or of sunshine can make the journey other than it is."

So he came to look closely at all things on the road. Day by day he read the lessons of the desert and the mountain. He learned to know directions by the growth of the trees. By the perfume of the lilies, he sought out the hidden springs. By the red

clouds at evening, he knew that the sky would be
fair. By the red light in the morning, he was
warned of the coming storm. And there were
many who followed him and his way, though he
did not will it so.

And he taught his companions, saying: "We
must seek his way in the nature of the things that
abide. To learn this nature of things is the beginning of wisdom. For day unto day uttereth speech,
and night unto night showeth knowledge. The way
of nature is solid, substantial, vast, and unchang-
ing. He who walks in it stands secure, as in the
shadow of a high tower or as if encompassed by a
mighty fortress. The wisdom of the forest shall be
granted to him who seeks for it with calm heart and
quiet eye."

But among his followers there were many who
were eager and would hasten on, and although they
spoke much of the Nature of Things and of the Law
of the Forest, they were contented with speaking.
"The road is long," they said to themselves, "and
the hours are fleeting." They had no time to con-
template the glory of the heavens. The beauty of
the lilies fell on unobservant eyes. For all these
things they trusted to the report of others. The
words passed from mouth to mouth, losing ever a

little of their truth. And in this wise the voice of wisdom was turned to the language of folly. For the nature of things is truth. But no man can find truth except he seek it for himself. And so they fared on, each well or ill, according to the truth to which his way bore witness.

Meanwhile those who bore the white banner remained long in council. At last one remembered that it was written, " Faith without works is dead, being alone." And it was written again, " Those who follow me in spirit must follow me in truth." The essence of truth lies not in thought or feeling, but must be expressed in deeds. Right feelings follow right actions. Thus it was with him; thus will it be with us.

Then they went their way together, doing good to one another. And each called his neighbor " brother"; and some bore cups of cold water, and some balm for healing; some carried oil and wine and pots of precious ointment. To whomsoever they met they gave help and comfort. The hungry they fed. The thirsty were given drink. He who had fallen by the wayside was lifted up and strengthened, and the blessing of cleanliness was brought to him who lay in filth and shame. The blessing of him that was ready to perish came upon them, and the heart of the widow sang for joy.

But soon those who were filled with zeal for good works were gathered together in great bands, and each band wished to magnify its work. In every way, to all men who asked, help was given. They searched out the lame and the blind, and brought them that they might perforce be healed. Cup after cup of cold water was given to the little ones, even to those who might bring water for themselves. They cared for the wounded wayfarer long after his wounds were made whole. It was their joy to bathe his limbs in oil and wine, or to swathe them in fragrant bands. And the wayfarer ceased to bear his own tent or to seek his own raiment. What others would do for him, he need not do for himself. And those who did not help themselves lost the power of self-help. And those who had helped others overmuch came themselves to need the help of others.

At last the number of the helpless became so great that there was no one to serve them. Many waited day after day for the aid that never came, and they grew so weak with waiting that they could not take up their burdens. The little ones were thrust aside by the strong, and as the band went on many of them were forgotten and left behind. They fainted and fell by the healing springs, because there was no one to give them drink, and they could not help themselves.

And the burden of the way grew very hard and grievous to bear. Then there were those who said that one cannot help another save by leading him to help himself. All that is given him must he repay. Sooner or later each must bear his own burden. Each must make his own way through the forest in such manner as he may.

So they turned back to the old Chart. They would read his words again, that they might be led to better deeds. In these words they found help and cheer. These words spake they one to another. They came like rain to a thirsty field, or as balm to a wound, or as good news from a far country. And there was wonderful consolation in the thought that for every step of the way he had spoken the right word.

So those who knew his words best were chosen as leaders, and great companies followed them. And as band after band passed along, his message sounded from one to another. His words were ever on their lips. Those who could run swiftly carried them far and wide, even into the depths of

the forest.   To those who were in sorrow they came
as glad tidings of great joy, and beautiful upon the
mountains seemed the feet of those who bore them.
Wherever men were weary and heavy laden, they
were cheered by his promise of rest.

.But there were some who turned to his message
only to gratify sordid hopes or vain desires.   He
who was lazy sought warrant for sleep.   He who
was covetous looked for gain.   He who was filled
with anger sought promise of vengeance.   There
were many who repeated his words for the mere
words' sake.   And there were some who used them
in disputations about the way.   And the words of
help on the Chart they turned into words of command.   Each one took these commands not to himself alone, but sought to enforce them upon others.
"For it is our duty," they said, "to see that no word
of his shall be unheeded of any man."   And many
rose in resistance.   And the conflicts on the way
were fierce and strong; for with each different band
there was diversity of interpretation.   Thus the
words of kindness became the voice of hate.

And it came to pass that all along the way the
green sward was red with the blood of wayfarers.
Everywhere the leaves of the forest were trampled
by struggling hosts.   And "In his name" was the

watchword of each warring band. And each band called itself "his army." And whosoever bore the sword that was reddest, they called the "Defender of the Faith." They placed his name upon their battle-flags, and beneath it they wrote these fearful words, "In this sign, conquer." And each went forth to conquer his neighbor, and the wayfarer fled from the sight of their banners as from a pestilence. But "Conquer, conquer," was no word of his. He spoke not of victory over others; only of conquest of oneself. He had said, "Resist not, but overcome evil with good." And till all men ceased to resist and ceased to conquer, no one found himself in the right way. Then some one said: "By words alone can no one truly follow him. His words without his faith and love are like sounding brass or tinkling cymbal. Out of the abundance of the heart the mouth speaketh. When the heart is empty the speech of the mouth is idle as the crackling of thorns beneath a pot."

And there appeared other bands from the number of those who had passed to the right of the first great rock; and seeing the tumult and confusion of the others, they said to themselves: "These are they who followed not us. We have chosen the better part. Our leader bears the only perfect

Chart. All other charts are the invention of men. In the right Chart there can be nothing false; in the others there can be nothing true. Those who have not the true Chart can never go right, not even for a moment. For even good deeds done in the paths of evil must partake of the nature of sin. Straight is the way and narrow is the gate, but there is no safety except ye walk therein."

So they went on, stumbling ever along the rocky road, never resting, never murmuring. "For the way at best is a vale of tears," said they, " and no one would have it otherwise. He found it thus in his time. He was ever a man of sorrows and acquainted with grief. More than all others had he suffered. It was his glory to be despised and rejected of men. For the greater the abasement the greater the exaltation in the land beyond the river." So day by day they walked in the hardest part of the road. But they spoke often together of a land of pure delight, of sweet fields beyond the swelling floods, and of turf soft as velvet that rose from the river's bank.

If perchance on the way they came to green pastures, they would hasten on, lest they should be tempted to rest before the day of rest was come. From sweet springs they turned aside, that theirs might be the greater satisfaction when they came to the sweetest springs of all. They shut their eyes to beauty and their ears to music, that the light and music of the unknown shore might burst upon them as a sudden revelation. They looked not at the stars, lest perchance these should declare a glory which was reserved for other days. Dreary and harsh was the way they trod. But in its very dreariness they found safety. They sought no pleasure, they fought no battles, they wasted no time. In the pushing aside of all temptation, the scorn of all beauty and idleness, they found delight. Against the strength of granite rock they set the force of iron will. Withal, at the bottom their hearts were light with the certainty of coming joy. Even the multitude of conflicting paths gave them a peculiar satisfaction; for whatever way they took was always the right way.

But there were some among them who lost all heart. And they threw their charts away and set forth in disorder through the forest and up the mountain. Some of them came safely to the river, far in advance of the bands they had left behind. But to most the way was strange, and harder than of old. And as the journey wore on they began to hate the forest and all its ways.

So they fared on, together or apart, in ever-deep-
ening shadow.   They distrusted their neighbors.
They despised the joyous bands who trooped after
their leaders with mouthing of verses and waving
of flags.   They were stirred by the sound of no
trumpet. They were deceived by no illusion of sunshine or of mist. They said: " We know the forest;
no one knows it but ourselves.   There is no future;
there is no way; there is no rest; there is no better
country. The azure mists are shadows only, hiding
some dreary plain, if haply they hide anything at
all.   Evil is man; evil are all things about him.
Love and joy, hope and faith, all these are but flick-
ering lights that lure him to destruction. Vultures
croak on the rocks. The fountains flow with ink.
Danger lurks in the desert.   The name of the river
is Death." And when they came to the shore of the
river they saw no rift in the clouds above it, for
their eyes were filled with gloom.

But as time passed on, the way of man grew
brighter, whether he would or no. No day nor
hour was without its joy to him who opened
his heart to receive it.   And men saw that
most of the difficulties and dangers of the way
were those which they unwittingly had made
for themselves or for others.   Thus, as the road

became more secure, it no longer seemed dreary or lonely.

And so it came to pass at last that men ceased to gather themselves in great bands. Nor did they longer set store on the sound of trumpets or the waving of flags. The men who were wisest ceased to be leaders of hosts. They became teachers and helpers instead.

And with all this a sure way was from day to day not hard to find. Men fell into it naturally and unconsciously. And the ways which are safe are innumerable as the multitude of those that may walk therein.

And those who had gone by diverse paths came from time to time together. Each praised the charms of the path he had taken, but each one knew that in other paths other men found as great delight. And as time went on many wise men passed over the way, and each in his own fashion left a record of all that had come to him.

But the old Chart men kept in ever-increasing reverence. They found that its simple, honest words were words of truth, and whoso sought for truth gained with it courage and strength. But they covered it no longer with their own additions and interpretations. Nor did any one insist that what he found helpful to himself should be law unto others. No longer did men say to one another, " This path have I taken ; this way must thou go."

And some one wrote upon the Chart this single rule of the forest: "Choose thou thine own best way, and help thy neighbor to find that way which for him is best." But this was erased at last; for beneath it they found the older, plainer words, which One in earlier times had written there, " *Thy neighbor as thyself.*"

THE STORY OF THE PASSION.

THE STORY OF THE PASSION.

THE Alps are not confined to Switzerland. They fill that little country full and overflow in all directions, into Austria, Italy, Germany, and France. Beautiful everywhere, these mountains are nowhere more charming than in Southern Bavaria. Grass-carpeted valleys, lakes as blue as the sky above them, dark slopes of pine and fir, overtopped by crags of gray limestone dashed by perpetual snow, the Bavarian Oberland is one of the most delightful regions in all Europe. When Attila and the Huns invaded Germany fifteen centuries ago, it is said that their cry was, "On to Bavaria — on to Bavaria! for there dwells the Lord God himself!"

In the heart of these mountains, shut off from the highways of travel by great walls of rock, lies the valley of the little river Ammer. Its waters are cold and clear, for they flow from mountain springs, and its willow-shaded eddies are full of trout. At first a brawling torrent, its current grows more gentle as the valley widens and the rocks recede, and at last the little river flows quietly with broad windings through meadows carpeted with flowers. On these meadows, a couple of miles apart, lie the twin villages of the Ammer Valley— the one world-famous, the other unheard of beyond the sound of its church-bells—Ober and Unter Ammergau.

Long, straggling, Swiss-like towns, these villages on the Ammer meadows are. You may find a hundred such between Innsbrück and Zurich. Stone houses, plastered outside and painted white, stand close together, each one passing gradually backward into woodshed, barn, and stable. You may lose your way in the narrow, crooked streets, as purposeless in their direction as the footsteps of the cows who first surveyed them.

Oberammergau is a cleaner town than most, with a handsomer church, and a general evidence of local pride and modest prosperity. Frescoes on the walls of the houses here and there, paintings of saints and angels, bear witness to a love of beauty and to the prevalence of a religious spirit. These pictures, still bright after more than a century's wear, go back to the time when the peasant boy, Franz Zwink, of Oberammergau, mixed paints for a famous artist who painted the interior of the Ettal

Monastery and the village church. The boy learned the art as well as the process, and when his master was gone, he covered the walls of his native town with pictures such as made men famous in other times and in other lands. The spirit of the Italian masters was his, and the work of Zwink at Oberammergau has been called "a wandering wave from the mighty sea of the Renaissance which has broken on a far-off coast."

The Passion Play at Oberammergau has been characterized as a relic of medieval times—the last remains of the old Miracle Play. This is true, in the sense of historical continuity, and in that sense alone. The spirit of the times has penetrated even to this isolated valley, and its Passion Play is as much a product of our century as the poetry of Tennyson. Miracle Plays were shown at Oberammergau and in the town about it more than five hundred years ago, but the Passion Play of to-day is not like them. The imps and devils and all the machinery of superstition are gone. Harmony has taken the place of crudity, and the Christ of Oberammergau is the Christ of modern conception. The Miracle Play, dead or dying everywhere else, has lived and been perfected at Oberammergau.

It has been pre-eminently the work of the Church

of Rome to teach the common people, and to train them to obedience. In its teaching it has made use of every means which could serve its purposes. Didactic teaching is not effective with tired and sleepy peasants. Sermons soothe, rather than instruct, after a week of hard labor in the fields. Hence comes the need of object-teaching, if teaching is to be real.

Images have been used in this way in the Catholic Church — not as objects to be worshiped, but as representations of sacred things. Paintings have served the same purpose. The noblest paintings in the world have been wrought to this end. It was in such lines alone that art could find worthy recognition. In like manner, processions and "Passion* Plays" have served the same purpose.

The old Miracle Plays were grotesque enough — made by common people for the instruction of common people. Even amid the pathos of divine suffering the peasants must be amused. Care was taken that the character of Judas should meet this demand. So Judas was made at once a traitor and a clown. His pathway was beset by devils of the most ridiculous sort. And when at last he hung

---

* The word "passion," as used in the term "Passionspiel," signifies anguish or sorrow. The Passion Play is the story of the great anguish.

himself on the stage, his body burst open, and the long links of sausages which represented intestines were devoured by the imps amid the laughter and delight of the peasant audience. Now all this has passed away. Wise and learned men have taken the play in hand, and have left it a monument to their piety and good taste. Everything grotesque, or barbarous, or ridiculous has been eliminated. All else is subordinated to a faithful and artistic representation of the life and acts of Christ. Stately prose and the language of the Gospel narratives have been substituted for doggerel verse. As a work of art, the Passion Play deserves a high place in the literature of Germany.

One striking feature of the Passion Play is the absence of superstitious elements. Beyond the dominating influence of the purpose of God, which is brought into strong prominence, there is almost nothing which suggests the supernatural or miraculous. That little even is forgotten in the intensity of human interest. The Devil and his machinations have vanished entirely. One sees in the religious customs of the people of Oberammergau few of the superstitions common among the peasant classes of other parts of Europe. In his little book, " Oberammergau und Seine Bewohner," Pastor

Daisenberger says: "Superstitious beliefs and customs one does not find here." Even the ordinary
ghost-stories and traditions of Germany are out-
worn and forgotten in this town.

In 1634, so the tradition says, the black death
came to Oberammergau, and one-tenth of the in-
habitants died. The others made a vow, "a trembling vow, breathed in a night of tears," that if God
should stay the plague, they would, on every tenth
year, repeat in full, for the edification of the people,
the Tragedy of the Passion. Other communities
might build temples or monasteries, or could undertake pilgrimages; it should be their duty to
show "The Way of the Cross." When this vow
was taken, the pestilence ceased, and not another
person perished. This was regarded by the people
as a visible sign of divine approval. Thus every
tenth year for nearly three centuries, ever since
the time when the Pilgrims landed on Plymouth
Rock, with varying fortunes and interruptions,
the Passion Play has been represented in Oberammergau.

The play in its present form is essentially the
work of Josef Alois Daisenberger, who was for
twenty years pastor of the church at Oberammergau. In this town he was born in the last year

of the last century, and there he died, in 1888, revered and beloved by all who came near him.

"I wrote the play," Pastor Daisenberger said, "for the love of my Divine Redeemer, and with no other object in view than the edification of the Christian world."

The first aim of the Passion Play has been the training of the common people. To its various representations came the peasants of Bavaria, Würtemberg, and the Tyrol, on horses, on donkeys, on foot, a long and difficult journey across mountain-walls and through great forests. It was the memory and inspiration of a lifetime to have seen the Passion Play.

About forty years ago the tourist world discovered this scene; and since then, on the decennial year, an ever-increasing interest has been felt, an ever-growing stream of travel has been turned toward the Ammer Valley. All, prince or peasant, are treated alike by the simple, honest people, and the same preparation is made for the reception of all. The purpose of the play should be kept in mind in any just criticism. To have the right to discuss it at all, one must treat it in a spirit of sympathy.

We came into Oberammergau on Friday, the 1st

day of August, 1890, to witness the performance of
the Sunday following. The city of Munich, seventy
miles away, was crowded with visitors, all bound
to the Passion Play. The express-train of twenty
cars which carried us from Munich was crowded
with people from almost every part of the civilized
world.

At Oberau, six miles from Oberammergau, at the
foot of the Ettal Mountain, we left the railway, and
there took part in a general scramble for seats in the
carriages. The fine new road winds through dark
pine woods, climbing the hill in long zigzags above
wild chasms, past the old monastery of Ettal, and
then slowly descends to the soft Ammer meadows.
The great peak of the Kofel is ever in front, while
the main chain of the Bavarian Alps closes the
view behind.

Arrived in the little village, all was bustle and
confusion. The streets were full of people — some
busy in taking care of strangers, others sauntering
idly about, as if at a country fair. Young women,
in black bodices and white sleeves, welcomed the
visitors at the little inns or served them in the
shops. Everywhere were young men in Tyrolese
holiday attire—green coats, black slouch hats, with
a feather or sprig of Edelweiss in the hat-band, and

with trousers, like those of the Scottish Highland-
ers, which end hopelessly beyond the reach of either
shoes or stockings. Besides the rustics and the
tourists, one met here and there upon the streets
men whose grave demeanor and long black hair
resting on their shoulders proclaimed them to be
actors in the Passion Play.

On Sunday morning we were awakened by the
sound of a cannon planted at the foot of the Kofel,
a sharp, conical, towering mountain, some two
thousand feet above the town, and bearing on its
summit a tall gilded cross. It was cold and rainy,
but that made no difference with the audience or
the play. At eight o'clock, when the cannon sounds
again, all are in their places, and the play begins.
It lasts for eight hours—from eight o'clock in the
morning to half-past five in the afternoon, with a
single interruption of an hour and a half at noon.
The stage is wide and ample. Its central part is
covered, but the front, which represents the fields
and the streets of Jerusalem, is in the open air.
This feature lends the play a special charm. On
the left, across the stage, over which the fitful rain-
clouds chase one another, we can plainly see the
long, green slope of Ettal mountain, dotted from
bottom to top with herdmen's huts or *châlets*, and

on the summit a tall pine-tree, standing out alone above all its brethren. On the other side appear the wild crags of the Kofel, its gilded cross glistening in the sunshine above the morning mists. Swallows fly in and out among the painted palm-trees, their twitter sounding sharply above the music of the chorus. The little birds raise their voices to make themselves heard to each other.

As the play progresses the intense truthfulness of the people of Oberammergau steadily grows upon us. For many generations the best intellects and noblest lives in the town have been devoted to the sole end of giving a worthy picture of the life and acts of Christ. Each generation of actors has left this picture more noble than it ever was before. Their work has been wrought in a spirit of serious truthfulness, which in itself places the Oberammergau stage in a class by itself, above and beyond all other theaters. Everything is real, and stands for what it is. Kings and priests are dressed, not in flimsy tinsel, but in garments such as real kings and priests may have worn. And so no artificial light or glare of fireworks is needed to make these costumes effective. And this genuineness enables these simple players to produce effects which the richest theaters would scarcely dare to undertake;

and all this in the open air, in glaring sunshine
or in pouring rain. The players themselves can
scarcely be called actors. In their way, they
are strong beyond all mere actors, and for this
reason — that they do not seem to act. From
childhood they have grown up in the parts they
play. Childish voices learn the solemn music
of the chorus in the schools, and childish forms
mingle in the triumphal procession in the regular
church festivals. All the effects of accumulated
tradition, all the results of years of training tend
to make of them, not actors at all, but living figures
of the characters they represent. And we can look
back over the history of Oberammergau, and see
how, through the growth of this purpose of its life,
it has come to be unique among all the towns of
Europe.

Many have wondered that in so small a town
there should be so many men of striking personality. The reason for this is to be sought in the
operation of natural selection. In the ordinary
German village, the best men find no career. They
go from home to the cities or to foreign lands, in
search of the work and influence not to be secured
at home. The strongest go, and the dull remain.
All this is reversed at Oberammergau. Only the

native citizen takes part in the play. Those who
are stupid or vicious are excluded from it. Not to
take part in the play is to have no reason for re-
maining in Oberammergau. To be chosen for an
important part is the highest honor the people
know. So the influences at work retain the best
and exclude the others. Moreover, the leading
families of Oberammergau, the families of Zwink,
Lang, Rendl, Mayr, Lechner, Diemer, etc., are
closely related by intermarriage. These people are
all of one blood — all of one great family. This
family is one of actors, serious, intelligent, devoted,
and all these virtues are turned to effect in their
acting.

This work is that of a lifetime. Little boys and
girls come on the stage in the arms of the mothers
— matrons of Jerusalem. Older boys shout in the
rabble and become at last Roman soldiers or servants of the High Priest. Still later, the best of
them are ranged among the Apostles, and the rare
genius becomes Pilate, John, Judas, or the Christ.

In the house of mine host, the chief of the
money-changers in the temple, the eldest daughter
was called Magdalena. In 1890, at fourteen, she
was leader of the girls in the tableau of the falling
manna. In 1900, she may, perhaps, become Mary

Magdalen, the end in life which her parents have chosen for her.

After the cannon sounds, the chorus of guardian spirits (*Schützengeister*) comes forward to make plain by speech or action the meaning of the coming scenes. This chorus is modeled after the chorus in the Greek plays. It is composed of twenty-four singers, the best that Oberammergau has, all picturesquely clad in Greek costumes,— white tunics, trimmed with gold, and over these an outer mantle of some deep, quiet shade, the whole forming a perfect harmony of soft Oriental colors. Stately and beautiful the chorus is throughout. The time which in ordinary theaters is devoted to the arranging of scenes behind a blank curtain is here filled by the songs and recitations of the guardian spirits. Once in the play the chorus appears in black, in keeping with the dark scenes they come forth to foretell. But at the end the bright robes are resumed, while the play closes with a burst of triumph from their lips.

At the beginning of each act, the leader of the singers, the village schoolmaster, comes forth from the chorus, and the curtain parts, revealing a tableau illustrative of the coming scenes. These tableaux, some thirty or forty in number, are taken

from scenes in the Old Testament which are supposed to prefigure acts in the life of Christ.   Thus
the treachery of Judas is prefigured by the sale of
Joseph by his brethren.   The farewell at Bethany
has its type in the mourning bride in the Song of
Solomon ; the Crucifixion, in the brazen serpent of
Moses.   Sometimes the connection between the tableaux and the scenes is not easily traced ; but even
then the pictures justify themselves by their own
beauty.   Often five hundred people are brought on
the stage at once.   These range in size from the
tall and patriarchal Moses to children of two years.
But, old or young, there is never a muscle or a fold
of garment out of place.   The first tableau represents Adam and Eve driven from Eden by the angel
with the flaming sword.   It was not easy to believe
that these figures were real.   They were as change-
less as wax.   They did not even wink.   The critic
may notice that the hands of the women are large
and brown, and the children's faces not free from
sunburn.   But there is no other hint that these
exquisite pictures are made up from the village
boys and girls, those who on other days milk the
cows and scrub the floors in the little town.   The
marvelously varied costumes and the grouping of
these tableaux are the work of the drawing-teacher,

Ludwig Lang. Without appearing anywhere in the play, this gifted man makes himself everywhere felt in the delicacy of his feeling for harmonies of color.

At the beginning of the play the leader of the chorus addresses the audience as friends and brothers who are present for the same reason as the actors themselves — namely, to assist devoutly at the mystery to be set forth, the story of the redemption of the world. The purpose is, as far as may be, to share the sorrows of the Saviour and to follow him step by step on the way of his sufferings to the cross and sepulcher. Then comes the prologue, solemnly intoned, of which the most striking words are these:

> "Nicht ewig zürnet Er
> Ich will, so spricht der Herr,
> Den Tod des Sünders nicht."

" He will not be angry forever. I, saith the Lord, will not the death of the sinner. I will forgive him; he shall live, and in my Son's blood shall be reconciled."

When its part is finished the chorus retires, and the Passion Play begins with the entry of Christ into Jerusalem. Far in the distance we hear the music, "Hail to thee, O David's son!" Then follows a seemingly endless procession of men, women, and children who wave palm-leaves and shout hosannas. One little flaxen-haired girl, dressed in blue, and carrying a long, slender palm-leaf, is especially striking in her beauty and naturalness.

At last He comes, riding sidewise upon a beast that seems too small for his great stature. He is dressed in a purple robe, over which is a mantle of rich crimson. Beside him, in red and olive-green, is the girlish-looking youth, Peter Rendl. who takes the part of Saint John. Behind him follow his disciples, each with the pilgrim's staff. Two of these are more conspicuous than the others. One is a white-haired, eager old man, wearing a mantle of olive-green. The other, younger, dark, sullen, and tangle-haired, dressed in a robe of saffron over dull yellow, is the only person in the throng out of harmony with the prevailing joyousness.

Followed by the people, who stand apart in reverence as he passes among them, Christ approaches the temple. His face is pale, in marked contrast to his abundant black hair. His expression is serious, or even care-worn, less mild than in the usual pictures of Jesus, but certainly in keeping with the scenes of the Passion Play. A fine, strong, mas-

PETER RENDL AS SAINT JOHN.

terful man of great stature and immense physical strength is the wood-carver, Josef Mayr, who now for three successive decades has taken this part. A man of attractive presence and lofty bearing, one whom every eye follows as he goes about the town on the round of his daily duties, yet simple-hearted and modest, as becomes one who takes on himself not only the dress but the name and figure of the Saviour.

Essays have been written on "Christus" Mayr and his conception of Jesus, and I can only assent to the general impression. To me it seems that Mayr's thought of Christ is one which all must accept. He appears as "one driven by the Spirit," — the great mild teacher, the man who can afford to be silent before kings and before mobs, and to whom the pains of Calvary are not more deep than the sorrows of Gethsemane, the man who comes to do the work of his Father, regardless alike of human praise or of human contempt. The great strength of the presentation is that it brings to the front the essentials of Christ's life and death. There is no suggestion of theological subtleties nor of the ceremonies of any church. It is simply true and terrible.

From one of his fellow-actors, I learned this of

Josef Mayr.   He has always been what he is now, a hand-worker ("*gemeiner Arbeiter*") in Oberammergau.   He has never been away from his native town except once, when he went as a workman to Vienna, and once when, in 1870, the play was interrupted by the war with France, and Mayr himself was taken into the army.   Out of respect to his art, he was never sent to the front, but kept in the garrison at Munich.   When the war was over, and he came back, in 1871, the grateful villagers resumed the play as their "best method of thanking God who had given them the blessings of victory and peace."

Canon Farrar, of Westminster, has given us the best and most sympathetic account yet published of the various actors.   Of Mayr he said: "It is no small testimony to the goodness and the ability of Josef Mayr that in his representation of Christ he does not offend us by a single word or a single gesture. If there were in his manner the slightest touch of affectation or of self-consciousness; if there were the remotest suspicion of a strut in his gait, we should be compelled to turn aside in disgust.   As it is, we forget the artist altogether.   For it is easy to see that Josef Mayr forgets himself, and wishes only to give a faithful picture of the events in the Gospel story."

As the Master enters the temple, he finds that its courts are filled with a noisy throng of money-changers, peddlers, and dealers in animals for sacrifice. He is filled with wrath and indignation. In a commanding tone, he orders them to take their own and leave this holy place. "There is room enough for trading outside. 'My house,' thus saith the Lord, 'shall be a house of prayer to all the people.' Ye have made it a den of thieves." ("*Zur Räuberhöhle, habt Ihr es gemacht!*")

The peddlers pay no attention to his protest. Then, with a sudden burst of wrath, he breaks upon them, overturning their tables, scattering their gold upon the floor, and beating them with thongs. The animals kept for sacrifice are released. The sheep scamper backward to the rear of the stage, and escape through the open door. The white doves fly out over the heads of the spectators, and are lost against the green slopes of the Kofel.

The play now follows the Gospel narrative very closely. It is, in fact, the Gospel story, with only such changes as fit it for continuous presentation. Events aside from the current of the story, such as the wedding at Cana and the raising of Lazarus, are omitted. There are few long speeches. The leading features of what may be called the plot, the wrath of the money-changers, the fierce hatred of the Pharisees, the avarice of Judas, which makes him their tool, are all sharply emphasized.

The next scene introduces us to the High Council of the Jews, and to its leading spirit, Caiaphas. Caiaphas is represented by the burgomaster of the village, Johann Lang. "No medieval pope," says Canon Farrar, "could pronounce his sentences with more dignity and verve. He is what has been called 'that terrible creature, the perfect priest.'" Violent, unforgiving, and harsh, he is the soul of the conspiracy. His strong determination is reflected in the weak malignity of his colleague, Annas, as well as in the priests and scribes. "While he lives," Caiaphas says, "there is no peace for Israel. It is better that one man should die, that the whole nation perish not."

We next behold Jesus accompanied by his disciples on the road toward the house of Simon of Bethany. As they walk along, he talks sadly of his approaching death. None of them can understand his words; for to them he has been victorious over all his enemies. "A word from thee," says Peter, "and they are crushed." "I see not," says Thomas, "why thou speakest so often of sorrow and death. Do we not read in the prophets that Christ lives forever? Thou canst not die, for with thy power thou wakest even the dead." Even John declares that Christ's words are dark and dismal, while he and his associates use every effort to cheer the Master.

At the house of Simon of Bethany, Mary Magdalen breaks the costly dish of ointment. Judas, who carries the slender purse of the disciples, is vexed at the waste, and talks of all the good the value of this ointment might have done if given to the poor.

Very carefully worked out is the character of Judas, represented by Johann Zwink, the miller of Oberammergau, who ten years ago took the part of Saint John. The people of Oberammergau regard Zwink as the most gifted of all their actors; for he can, they say, play any part. (" *Er spielt alle Rolle.*") Gregor Lechner, who in his younger days had the part of Judas, is now Simon of Bethany. Of all the actors of Oberammergau, the people told us, Lechner is the most beloved (" *bestens beliebt*").

In Zwink's conception, Judas is a man full of ambition, but without enthusiasm. He is attracted by the power of Christ, from which he expects great results. But Christ seems to care little for his own mighty works. " My mission," he says, "is not to command, but to serve." So Judas becomes impatient and dissatisfied. The eager enthusiasm of Peter and the tender devotion of John alike bore and disgust him. So the emissaries of Caiaphas find him half-prepared for their mission. He admits that he has made a mistake in joining his fortunes to those of an unpractical and sorrowful prophet who lets great opportunities slip from his grasp, and who wastes a fortune in precious ointment with no more thought than if it had been water. "There has of late been a coolness between him and me," he confesses. "I am tired," he says, "of hoping and waiting, with nothing before me except poverty, humiliation, perhaps even torture and the prison." He is especially ill at ease when the Master speaks of his approaching death. "If thou givest up thy life," he says, "what will become of us?" And so Judas reasons with himself that he can afford to be prudent. If his Master fail, then he must be a false prophet, and there is no use in following him. If he succeed, as with his mighty power he can hardly fail to do, then, says Judas, "I will throw myself at his feet. He is such a good man; never have I seen him cast a penitent away. But I fear to face the Master. His sharp look goes through and through me. Still at the most I shall

JOHANN ZWINK AS JUDAS.

only tell the priests where my Master is." And thus the good and bad impulses struggle for the mastery, giving to this character the greatest tragic interest. He visibly shrinks before the words of Christ, " One of you shall betray me." In the High Council he cringes under the scorching reproach of Nicodemus. " Dost thou not blush," Nicodemus says, " to sell thy Lord and Master? This blood-money calls to heaven for revenge. Some day it will burn hot in thine avarice-sunken soul."

But the High Priest says, " Come, Judas, take the silver, and be a man." And when the thirty pieces are counted out to him, he cannot resist the temptation, but clutches them with a miser's grasp and hurries off to intercept the Master on his way through the Garden of Gethsemane. Meanwhile, after a tender farewell from his mother, Christ leaves the house of Simon of Bethany, and, with his disciples, takes the road to Jerusalem.

The part of Mary the mother of Christ is admirably taken by Rosa Lang. In dress and mien, she seems to have stepped down from some picture-frame of Raphael or Murillo. The Mary of Rosa Lang is in every respect a worthy companion of Mayr's Christus.

The various scenes in which the Apostles appear

are modeled more or less after the great religious paintings, especially those of the Bavarian artist, Albrecht Dürer. The Last Supper is a living representation of the famous painting of Leonardo da Vinci in the refectory at Milan. Peter and Judas are here brought into sharp contrast. Next to Christ, is the slender figure of the beloved disciple. The characters of the different Apostles are placed in bold relief. We are at once interested in the fine face of Andreas Lang, the Apostle Thomas, critical and questioning, but altogether loyal. The Apostle Philip looks for signs and visions, and would see the Father coming in His glory from the skies, not in the common every-day scenes of life into which the Master led them. "Have I been so long time with thee, and yet hast thou not known me, Philip?"

Next comes the night scene in the Garden of Gethsemane on the Mount of Olives. The tired Apostles rest upon the grassy bank, and one by one they fall asleep. Even Peter, who is nearest the Master, can keep awake no longer. Christ kneels upon the rocks above the sleeping Peter. "O Father, if it be possible, let this cup pass from me." He looks back to his disciples. "Are your eyes so heavy that ye cannot watch? The weight of God's

ROSA LANG AS MARY.

justice lies upon me. The sins of the fallen world weigh me down. O Father, if it is not possible that this hour go by, then may thy holy will be done."

Suddenly a great tumult is heard. The faint light of the morning is reflected from the clanging armor and from glittering spears. The Apostles are rudely awakened. Judas comes forth and greets the Master with a kiss. At this signal, the Master is seized by the soldiers and roughly bound. Then he is carried away, first to Annas, and afterwards to the house of Caiaphas.

Of the scenes that immediately follow, the most striking is that of the denial of Peter. Peter, as represented by the sexton of the church, Jacob Hitt, is an old man with a young heart, eager and impulsive. He dreams of the noble part he will take while standing by the Master's side before kings and priests, but behaves very humanly when he is brought face to face with an unexpected test.

The scenes of the night have crowded thick and fast. The Apostles have been scattered by the soldiers. The Master had been bound, and carried away they know not whither. Peter had tried to defend him, but was told to "put away his useless sword." In forlorn agony Peter and John wander about in the dark, seeking news of Jesus. They

meet a servant who tells them that he has been carried before the High Priest, and that the whole
brood of his followers is to be rooted out.

Near the house of the High Priest Annas we see
a sort of inn occupied by rough soldiers. The night
is damp and cold. A maid has kindled a fire in the
courtyard, and Peter approaches it to warm his
hands, and, if possible, to gain some further news
of the Master. He hears the soldiers talking of
Malchus, one of their number who had had his ear
cut off. They boast of what they will do with the
culprit, if he should ever fall into their power. "An
ear for an ear," he hears them say. Suddenly the
maid turns towards Peter and says, "Yes, you,
surely you were with the Nazarene Jesus." Peter
hestitates. Should he confess, he would have his
own ears cut off, an ear for an ear—and most likely
his head, too, while his body would be thrown out
on the rubbish heap behind the inn. Peter had
said that he would die for the Master; and so he
would on the field of battle, or in any way where
he might have a glorious death. He would die for
the Master, but not then and there. The death of
a martyr has its pleasures, no doubt, but not the
death of a dog.

While Peter stood thus considering these matters,

one and then another of the servants insisted that
he had surely been seen with the Nazarene Jesus.
Again and again Peter refused all knowledge of the
Master. When the cock crew once more he had
denied his Master thrice. While Peter still insisted,
the door opened and the Master came forth under
the High Priest's sentence of death. "And the
Lord turned and looked upon Peter, and Peter went
out and wept bitterly." "Oh, Master," he says in
the play:

> "Oh, Master, how have I fallen!
> I have denied thee, how can it be possible?
> Three times denied thee! Oh, thou knowest, Lord,
> I was resolved to follow thee to death."

Meanwhile Judas hears the story of what has
happened. He is at once filled with agony and
remorse, for he had not expected it. He was sure
that the great power of the Master would bring
him through safely at last. In helpless agony, he
rushes before the Council and makes an ineffective
protest. "No peace for me forevermore; no peace
for you," he says. "The blood of the innocent
cries aloud for justice." He is repulsed with cold
indifference. Will it or not," says the High Priest,
"he must die, and it would be well for thee to look
out for thyself."

In fury he cries out, "If he dies, then am I a traitor. May ten thousand devils tear me in pieces! Here, ye bloodhounds, take back your curse!" And flinging the blood-money at the feet of the priests, he flies from their presence, pursued by the specter of his crime.

The next scene shows us the field of blood — a wind-swept desert, with one forlorn tree in the foreground. We see the wretched Judas before the tree. He tears off his girdle, "a snake," he calls it, and places it about his neck, snapping off a branch of the tree in his haste to fasten it. "Here, accursed life, I end thee; let the most miserable of all fruit hang upon this tree." In the action we feel that Judas is not so much wicked as weak. He has little faith and little imagination, and his folly of avarice hurries him into betrayal. Those who see the play feel as the actors feel, that Christ knows the weakness of man. He would have forgiven Judas, just as he forgave Peter.

In the early morning Christ is brought before Pontius Pilate. The Roman governor, admirably represented by Thomas Rendl, appears in the balcony and talks down to Caiaphas, who sends up his accusations from the street below. His clear sense of justice makes Pilate at first more than a match for the conspirators. With magnificent scorn he tells Caiaphas that he is "astounded at his sudden zeal for Cæsar." Of Christ he says: "He seems to me a wise man — so wise that these dark men cannot bear the light from his wisdom." Learning that Jesus is from Galilee, he throws the whole matter into the hands of Herod, the governor of that province.

The words of Pilate are very finely spoken. "We marvel," says one writer, "how the peasant Rendl learned to bear himself so nobly or to utter the famous question, 'What is truth?' with a certain dreamy inward expression and tone, as though outward circumstances had for the instant vanished from his mind, and he were alone with his own soul and the flood of thought raised by the words of Jesus."

In contrast to Pilate, stands Herod, lazy and voluptuous. He, too, finds nothing of evil in Jesus, whom he supposes to be a clever magician. "Cause that this hall may become dark," he says, "or that this roll of paper, which is thy sentence of death, shall become a serpent." He receives Christ in good-natured expectancy, which changes to disgust when he answers him not a word. Herod pronounces him "dumb as a fish," and, after clothing

him in a splendid purple mantle, he sends him
away unharmed, with the title of "King of Fools."

Again Christ is brought before Pilate, who tells
Caiaphas plainly that his accusations mean only
his own personal hatred, and that the voice of
the people is but the senseless clamor of the mob
set in operation by intrigue. Pilate orders Jesus
to be scourged, in the hope that the sight of his
noble bearing amid unmerited cruelties may soften
the hearts of the people. Nowhere does the noble
figure of Mayr appear to better advantage than
in this scene, where, after a brutal chastisement,
scarcely lessened in the presentation on the stage,
the Roman soldiers place a cattail flag in his hand
and salute him as a king.

Pilate then brings forth an abandoned wreck of
humanity, old Barabbas, the murderer. As Christ
stands before them, blood-stained and crowned with
thorns, half in hope and half in irony, Pilate invites
them to choose. "Behold the man," he said, "a
wise teacher whom ye have long honored, guilty
of no evil deed. Jesus or Barabbas, which will ye
choose?"

All the more fiercely the mob cries, "Crucify him!
Crucify him!"

Pilate is puzzled. "I cannot understand these

"ECCE HOMO!"

people," he said. "But a few days ago, ye followed this man with rejoicing through the streets of Jerusalem." The High Priest threatens to appeal to Rome. Pilate fears to face such an appeal. He has little confidence in the favor or the justice of the Cæsar whom he serves. At last he consents to what he calls "a great wrong in order to avert a greater evil." He calls for water, and washes his hands in ostentatious innocence. Finally, as he signs the verdict of condemnation in wrath and disgust, he breaks his staff of office, and flings the fragments upon the stairs, at the feet of the priests.

Next we behold in the foreground of the stage, John and Mary the mother of Jesus, and with them a little group of followers. A tumult is heard, and, in the midst of a great throng of people, we see three crosses borne by prisoners. Jesus beholds his mother. Suddenly he faints, under the weight of the cross. The rough soldiers urge him on. Simon of Cyrene, a sturdy passer-by, who is carrying home provisions from the market, is seized by the soldiers and forced to give aid. At first he refuses. "I will not do it," he says; "I am a free man, and no criminal." But his indignant protests turn to pity, when he beholds the Holy Man of Nazareth. "For the love of thee," he says, "will I bear thy cross. Oh, could I make myself thus worthy in thy sight!"

The closing scenes of the Passion Play, associated as they are with all that has been held sacred by our race for nearly two thousand years, are thrilling beyond comparison. No one can witness them unmoved. No one can forget the impression made by the living pictures. In simplicity and reverence, the work is undertaken, and it awakens in the beholder only corresponding feelings. Every heart, for the time at least, is stirred to its depths.

When the curtain rises, two crosses are seen, each in its place. The central cross is not yet raised. The Roman soldiers take their time for it. "Come, now," says one of them, "we must put this Jewish king upon his throne." So the heavy cross, with its burden, is raised in its place. We see the bloody nails in his hands and feet; and so realistic is the representation, that the nearest spectator cannot see that he is not actually nailed to the cross. There is no haste shown in the presentation. The Crucifixion is not a tableau, displayed for an instant and then withdrawn. The scene lasts so long that one feels a strange sense of surprise when Christus Mayr appears alive again.

Twenty minutes is the time actually taken for the

representation. "It is hard," said our landlady, the good Frau Wiedermann, "to be on the cross so long, even if one is not actually nailed to it. It is hard for the thieves, too," she said, "as well as for Josef Mayr."

The thieves themselves deserve a moment's notice. The one on the right is a bald old man, who meets his death in patience and humility. The one on the left is a robust young fellow, who defies his associates and tormentors alike, and joins his voice to that of the rabble in scoffing at the power of Jesus. "If thou be a god," he says, "save thyself and us." There is at first a struggle over the inscription at the head of the cross. "Let it read, 'He called himself the King of the Jews,'" say the priests. But the Roman soldier is obdurate. "What I have written I have written," and the centurion grimly nails it on the cross above his head, regardless alike of their rage and protestations.

Meanwhile, in the foreground the four Roman guards part the purple robe of Christ, each one taking his share. But the seamless coat they will not divide. So they cast the dice on the ground to see to whom this prize shall fall. They are in no hurry. Traitors and thieves have all night to die in, and they can wait for them. The first soldier throws a low number, and gives up the contest. The second does better. The third calls up to the cross, "If thou be a god, help me to throw a lucky number." One cast of the dice is disputed. It has to be tried again.

Meanwhile we hear the poor dying body on the cross, in a voice broken with agony, "Father, forgive them, for they know not what they do." Again, amid the railings of the Jews, "My God, my God, why hast thou forsaken me?" Then again, after a sharp cry of pain, "It is finished!"

The captain drives the scoffing mob away, bidding the women come nearer. Then a Roman soldier, sent by Pilate, comes and breaks the legs of the thieves. We hear their bones crack under the club. Their heads fall, their muscles shrink, as the breath leaves the body. But finding that Jesus is already dead, the soldier breaks not his legs, but thrusts a spear into his side. We can see the spear pierce the flesh, but we cannot see that the blood flows from the spear-point itself, and not from the Master's body. The soldiers fall back with a feeling of awe. Then, one by one, as the darkness falls, we see them file away on the road to Jerusalem, and the Son of Man is left in silence.

Then follows the descent from the cross, which

suggests comparison with Rubens' famous painting in the Cathedral at Antwerp, but here shown with a fineness of touch and delicacy of feeling which that great painter of muscles and mantles could never attain. We see Nicodemus climb the ladder leaned against the back of the cross. He takes off first the crown of thorns. It is laid silently at Mary's feet. He pulls out the nails one by one. We hear them fall upon the ground. With the last one falls the wrench with which he has drawn it. Passing a long roll of white cloth over each arm of the cross, he lets the Saviour down into the strong arms of Joseph of Arimathea, and, at last, into the loving embrace of John and Mary. No description can give an idea of the all-compelling force of this scene. A treatment less reverent than is given by these peasants would make it an intolerable blasphemy. As it is, its justification is its perfection.

And this is the justification of the Passion Play itself. It can never become a show. It can never be carried o other countries. It never can be given under other circumstances. So long as its players are pure in heart and humble in spirit, so long can they keep their well-earned right to show to the world the Tragedy of the Cross.

THE CALIFORNIA OF THE PADRE.

THE CALIFORNIA OF THE PADRE.*

THERE is something in the name of Spain which calls up impressions rich, warm, and romantic. The "color of romance," which must be something between the hue of a purple grape and the red haze of the Indian summer, hangs over everything Spanish. Castles in Spain have ever been the fairest castles, and the banks of the Xenil and the Guadalquivir still bound the dream-land of the poet.

> "There was never a castle seen
> So fair as mine in Spain;
> It stands embowered in green,
> Overlooking a gentle slope,
> On a hill by the Xenil's shore."

It has been said of Spanish rule in California, that its history was written upon sand, only to be washed away by the advancing tide of Saxon civilization. So far as the economic or political development of our State is concerned, this is true;

---

* Address at the Teachers' Institute at Monterey, California, September, 1893.

the Mission period had no part in it, and its heroes have left no imperishable monuments.

But in one respect our Spanish predecessors have had a lasting influence, and the debt we owe to them, as yet scarcely appreciated, is one which will grow with the ages. It is said that Father Crespi, in 1770, gave Spanish names to every place where he encamped at night, and these names, rich and melodious, make the map of California unique among the States of the Union. It is fitting that the most varied, picturesque, and lovable of all the States should be the one thus favored. We feel everywhere the charm of the Spanish language — Latin cut loose from scholastic bonds, with a dash of firmness from the Visigoth and a touch of warmth from the sun-loving Moor. The names of Mariposa, San Buenaventura, Santa Barbara, Santa Cruz, and Monterey can never grow mean or common. In the counties along the coast, there is scarcely a hill, or stream, or village that does not bear some melodious trace of Spanish occupation.

To see what California might have been, we have only to turn away from the mission counties to the foothills of the Sierras, where the mining-camps of the Anglo-Saxon bear such names as Fiddletown, Red Dog, Dutch Flat, Murder Gulch, Ace of Spades,

or Murderer's Bar; these changing later, by euphe-
mistic vulgarity, into Ruby City, Magnolia Vale,
Largentville, Idlewild, and the like. Or, if not
these, our Anglo-Saxon practically gives us, not
Our Lady of the Solitude, nor the City of the Holy
Cross, not Fresno, the ash, nor Mariposa, the butter-
fly, but the momentous repetition of Smithvilles,
Jonesboroughs, and Brownstowns, which makes the
map of the Mississippi Valley a waste of unpoetical
mediocrity.

So the Spanish names constitute our legacy from
the Mission Fathers. It is now nearly three hundred and fifty years since Alta California was discovered, one hundred and twenty years since it was
colonized by white people, and a little over forty
years since it became a part of our republic. In
1542, Cabrillo had sailed up the coast as far as
Cape Mendocino. In 1577, Sir Francis Drake came
as far north as Point Reyes, where, seeing the
white cliffs of Marin County, he called the country
New Albion. Better known than these to Spanish-
speaking people was the voyage of Sebastian Vizcaino, who, in 1602, had coasted along as far as Point
Reyes, and had left a full account of his discoveries.
The landlocked harbor which Cabrillo had named
San Miguel, Vizcaino re-christened in honor of his

flag-ship, San Diego de Alcalá. Farther north, Vizcaino found a glorious deep and sheltered bay, "large enough to float all the navies of the world," he said; and this, in honor of the Viceroy of Mexico, he called the Bay of Monterey. To a broad curve of the coast to the north, between Point San Pedro and Point Reyes, he gave the name of the Bay of San Francisco,* dedicating it to the memory of St. Francis of Assisi. A rough chart of the coast was made by his pilot, Cabrera Bueno, who left also an account of its leading features.

For a hundred and sixty years after Vizcaino's expedition, no use was made of his discoveries. In Professor Blackmar's words: "During all this time, not a European boat cut the surf of the northwest coast; not a foreigner trod the shore of Alta California. The white-winged galleon, plying its trade between Acapulco and the Philippines, occasionally passed near enough so that those on board might catch glimpses of the dark timber-line of the mountains of the coast or of the curling smoke of the forest fires; but the land was unknown to them, and the natives pursued their wandering life unmolested."

Toward the end of the seventeenth century,

---

*This stretch of water, as explained below, lies entirely outside of what is now known as San Francisco Bay.

Father Salvatierra, head of the Jesuit missions in Lower California, fixed his eye on this region, and made plans for its occupation. In this the good Father Kühn — a German from Bavaria, whom the Spaniards knew as "Quino,"—seconded him. But these plans came to naught. The power of the Jesuit order was broken; the charge of the missions in Lower California was given to the Dominicans, that of Upper California to the Franciscans, and to these and their associates the colonization of California is due. The Franciscans, it is said, "were the first white men who came to live and die in Alta California."

And this is how it came about. One hundred and thirty years ago, the port of La Paz, in Baja California, lay baking in the sun. La Paz was then, as now, a little old town, with narrow, stony streets and adobe houses, standing amidst palms, and chaparral, and cactus. To this port of La Paz came, one eventful day, Don José de Galvez, envoy of the King of Spain. He brought orders to the Governor of California, Don Gaspar de Portolá, that he should send a vessel in search of the ports of San Diego and of Monterey, on the supposed island, or peninsula, of Upper California, once found by Vizcaino, but lost for a century and a half. There they were to establish colonies and missions of the Holy Catholic Church. They were "to spread the Catholic religion," said the letter, "among a numerous heathen people, submerged in the obscure darkness of paganism, thereby to extend the dominion of the king, our lord, and to protect this peninsula of California from the ambitious designs of the foreign nations."

"The land must be fertile for everything," says Galvez, "for it lies in the same latitude as Spain." So they carried all sorts of household and field utensils, and seeds of every useful plant that grew in Spain and Mexico — the olive and the pomegranate, the grape and the orange, not forgetting the garlic and the pepper. All these were placed in two small ships, the San Carlos, under the gallant Captain Vila, and the San Antonio, under Captain Perez.

Padre Junípero Serra, chief apostle of these Spanish missions, blessed the vessels and the flags, commending the whole enterprise to the Most Holy Patriarch San José, who was supposed to feel a special interest in this class of expeditions. His early flight into Egypt gave him a peculiar fondness for schemes involving foreign travel. Galvez exhorted the soldiers and sailors to respect the priests, and not to quarrel with each other. And thus they sailed away for San Diego in the winter of 1769.

At the same time there was organized a land expedition, which should cross the sandy deserts and cactus-covered hills and join the vessels at San Diego. That there should be no risk of failure, Don Gaspar de Portolá divided the land forces into two divisions, one led by himself, the other by Captain Rivera. These two parties were to take different routes, so that if one were destroyed the other might accomplish the work. In front of each band were driven a hundred head of cattle, which were to colonize the new territories with their kind.

Padre Serra went with the land expedition under the command of Portolá. A barefooted friar, clad in a rough cloak confined by a rope at the waist, looks comfortable enough in the cool shade of an Italian cathedral; but the garb of the Franciscan order is ill-fitted to the peculiarities of the California *mesa*. For the vegetation of Lower California makes up in bristliness what it lacks in luxuriance. Bush cactuses, so prickly that it makes one's eyes smart to look at them, and bunch cactuses, in wads of thorns as large as a bushel-basket, swarm everywhere. Before the barefooted Padre had traveled far, so Miss Graham tells us in her charming little paper on the Spanish missions, he had made the acquaintance of many species of cactus. Horses in that country become lame sometimes, and people say that they are "cactus-legged." And soon Father Serra became "cactus-legged," too, so that he could neither walk nor ride a mule. The Indians were therefore obliged to carry him in a litter, for he would not go back to La Paz.

But the Father felt great compassion for the Indians, who had enough to do to carry themselves. He prayed fervently for a time, and then, according to the chronicler of the expedition, "He called a mule-driver and said to him: 'Son, do you know some remedy for my foot and leg?' But the mule-driver answered, 'Father, what remedy can I know? Am I a surgeon? I am a mule-driver, and have cured only the sore backs of beasts.' 'Then consider me a beast,' said the Father, 'and this sore leg to be a sore back, and treat me as you would a mule.' Then said the muleteer, 'I will, Father, to please you,' and taking a small piece of tallow, he mashed it between two stones, mixing with it herbs that grew close by. Then heating it over the fire, he anointed the foot and leg, and left the plaster upon the sore. 'God wrought in such a manner,' wrote to Padre Serra afterwards, 'that I slept all that night, and awoke so much relieved that I got up and said matins and prime, and afterwards mass, as if nothing had happened.'"

But Father Serra did not show his faith by such simple miracles as these alone. In one of his revival meetings in Mexico, Bancroft tells us, he was beating himself with a chain in punishment for his imaginary offenses, when a man seized the chain and beat himself to death as a miserable sinner, in the presence of the people. At another time, sixty persons who neglected to attend his meetings were killed by an epidemic, and the disease went on, killing one after another, until the people had been scared into attention to their religious duties. Then, at a sign from Padre Serra, the plague abated.

At one time the good Padre was well lodged and entertained in a very neat wayside cottage on a desolate and solitary road. Later he learned that there was no such cottage in that region, and, we are told, he concluded that his entertainers were Joseph, Mary, and Jesus.

Suffering greatly from thirst on one of his journeys, he said to his companions, who were complaining: "The best way to prevent thirst is to eat little and talk less." In a violent storm he was perfectly calm, and the storm ceased instantly when a saint chosen by lot had been addressed in prayer. And so on; for miracles like these are constant accompaniments of a mind wholly given over to religious enthusiasm.

In due season, Padre Serra and his party arrived at San Diego, having followed the barren and dreary coast of Lower California for three hundred and sixty miles, often carrying water for great distances, and as often impeded by winter rains. The boats and the other party were already there, and in the valley to the north of the *mesa,* on the banks of the little San Diego River, they founded the first mission in California.

Within a fortnight of Serra's arrival at San Diego, a special land expedition set out in search of Vizcaino's lost port of Monterey. The expedition, under Don Gaspar de Portolá, was unhappy in some respects, though fortunate in others — unhappy, for after wandering about in the Coast Range for six months, the soldiers returned to San Diego, weary, half-starved, and disgusted, failing altogether, as they supposed, to find Monterey; fortunate, for it was their luck to discover the far more important Bay of San Francisco. It seems evident, from the researches of John T. Doyle and others, that the company of Portolá, from the hills above what is now Redwood City, were the first white men to behold the present Bay of San Francisco. The journal of Miguel Costanzo, a civil engineer with Portolá's command, is still preserved in the Sutro Library in San Francisco, and Costanzo's map of the coast has been published. The diary of Father Crespi, who accompanied Portolá, has also been printed.

The little company went along the coast from San Diego northward, meeting many Indians on the way, and having various adventures with them. In the pretty valley which they named San Juan Capistrano, they found the Indian men dressed in suits of paint, the women in bearskins. On the site of the present town of Santa Ana, which they called Jesus de los Temblores, they met terrific earthquakes day and night. At Los Angeles, they celebrated the feast of Our Lady the Queen of the Angels (*Nuestra Señora, Reina de Los Angeles*), from which the valley took the name it still bears. They passed up the broad valley of San Fernando Rey, and crossed the mountains to the present village of Saugus. Thence they went down the Santa Clara River to San Buenaventura and Santa Bar-

bara, their route coinciding with that of the present
railroad. Above San Buenaventura they found
Indians living in huts of sagebrush. At Santa
Barbara, the Indians fed on excellent fish, but
played the flute at night so persistently that Portolá
and his soldiers could not sleep for the music.
They next passed Point Concepcion, and crossed
the picturesque Santa Ynez and the fertile Arroyo
Grande to the basin-shaped valley of San Luis
Obispo, with its row of four conical mountains.
At the last of these, Moro Rock, they reached the
sea again. Above Piedras Blancas, where the
rugged cliffs of the Santa Lucía crowd down to the
ocean, they were blocked, and could go no farther.
Crossing the mountains to the east, they followed
Nacimiento Creek to below Paso Robles, then went
down the dusty valley of the Salinas, past the
pastures on which the missions of San Miguel and
Soledad were later planted. Below Soledad, they
came again to the sea. They then went along
the shore to the westward, past the present site of
Monterey and Pacific Grove, and on to the Point
of Pines itself, the southern border of the Bay of
Monterey. Yet not one of them recognized the bay
or any of the landmarks described by Vizcaino. At
the Point of Pines, they were greatly disheartened,

205

En 3 de Junio de 1784 en la Yglesia de esta Mission de Carmelo de
Monterrey, previas las Convenientes Instruccion, renovacion segun
fronterisos, previas las Instruccion de su Ygnacia el contracto Matrimo-
nio con...

... y en virtud de ... Cartas Celebrado ... entre Obligados los dos
con ... el Ygnacia Cartas Celebrado ... Ygna ... y en virtud ... en
... el Bagtizo ... en ... desposado en
Conculla ... Cristiana y Cartas presente los desposados Y
Cartas Y ... Cristiana Maria ... como ... como 6 50 años
... y padre Christianos ambos a fin...
... y ... Christianos ... y padres ...
... y ... libros y ... y con su nombre
... con ... firmado. Fray

Fr. Junipero Serra

En 3 de Junio de 1784 en la Yglesia de esta Mission de Carmelo de
Monterrey, despues de convenientes instruidos, y y ... por ser
los Christianos Ritos y orden de N. S. Yglesia, El Matrimonial Contracto...

because they could nowhere find a trace of the Bay of Monterey, or of any other bay which was sheltered, or on which "the navies of the world could ride." Father Crespi celebrated here "the Feast of Our Father in the New World"; "or," he adds, "perhaps in a corner of the Old World, without any other church or choir than a desert." Portolá offered to return, but Crespi said : "Let us continue our journey until we find the harbor of Monterey; if it be God's will, we will die fulfilling our duty to God and our country." So they crossed the Salinas again, and went northward along the shore of the very bay they had sought so long. Then they came to another river, where they killed a great eagle, whose wings spread nine feet and three inches. They called this river Pajaro, which means "bird," and devoutly added to it the name of Saint Anne, " Rio del Pajaro de Santa Ana." To the memory of this bird, the Pajaro River still remains dedicated. Farther on, they came to forests of redwood—"*Palo colorado,*" they called it. Crespi describes the trees "as very high, resembling cedars of Lebanon, but not of the same color; the leaves different, and the wood very brittle."

At Santa Cruz, on the San Lorenzo River, they encamped, still bewailing their inability to find

Monterey Bay. Going northward, along the coast past Pescadero and Halfmoon Bay, they saw the great headland of Point San Pedro. They called it Point Guardian Angel (*Angel Custodio*), and from its heights they could clearly see Point Reyes and the chalk-white islands of the Farallones. These landmarks they recognized from the charts of Cabrera Bueno. Crespi says: "Scarce had we ascended the hill, when we perceived a vast bay formed by a great projection of land extending out to sea. We see six or seven islands, white, and differing in size. Following the coast toward the north, we can perceive a wide, deep cut, and north-west we see the opening of a bay which seems to go inside the land. At these signs, we come to recognize this harbor. It is that of our Father St. Francis, and that of Monterey we have left behind." "But some," he adds, " cannot believe yet that we have left behind us the harbor of Monterey, and that we are in that of San Francisco."

But the " Harbor of San Francisco," as indicated by Cabrera Bueno, lay quite outside the Golden Gate, in the curve between Point San Pedro on the south, and Point Reyes on the north. The exist-ence of the Golden Gate, and the landlocked waters within, forming what is now known as San Fran-

cisco Bay, was not suspected by any of the early
explorers. The high coast line, the rolling break-
ers, and, perhaps, the banks of fog, had hidden the
Golden Gate and the bay from Cabrillo, Drake, and
Vizcaino alike. By chance a few members of Portolá's otherwise unfortunate expedition discovered
the glorious harbor. Some of the soldiers, led by
an officer named Ortega, wandered out on the
Sierra Morena, east of Point San Pedro. When
they reached the summit and looked eastward, an
entirely new prospect was spread out before them.
From the foothills of these mountains, they saw a
great arm of the ocean — "a mediterranean sea,"
they termed it, according to Mr. Doyle's account,
" with a fair and extensive valley bordering it, rich
and fertile — a paradise compared with the country they had been passing over." They rushed
back to the seashore, waving their hats and shout-
ing. Then the whole party crossed over from Halfmoon Bay into the valley of San Mateo Creek.
Thence they turned to the south to go around the
head of the bay, passing first over into the Cañada
del Raymundo, which skirts the foot of the mountain. Soon they came down the " Bear Gulch " to
San Francisquito Creek, at the point where Sears-
ville once stood, before the great Potolá Reservoir

covered its traces and destroyed its old landmark, the Portolá Tavern. They entered what is now the University Campus, on which columns of ascending smoke showed the presence of many camps of Indians. These Indians were not friendly. The expedition was out of provisions, and many of its members were sick from eating acorns. There seemed to be no limit to the extension of the Estero de San Francisco. At last, in despair, but against the wishes of Portolá, they decided to return to San Diego. They encamped on San Francisquito Creek, and crossed the hills again to Halfmoon Bay. Then they went down the coast by Point Año Nuevo, to Santa Cruz. At the Point of Pines they spent two weeks, searching again everywhere for the Bay of Monterey.

At last they decided that Vizcaino's description must have been too highly colored, or else that the Bay of Monterey must, since his time, have been filled up with silt or destroyed by some earthquake. At any rate, the bay between Santa Cruz and the Point of Pines was the only Monterey they could find. According to Washburn, Vizcaino's account was far from a correct one. It was no fault of Portolá and Crespi that, after spending a month on its shores, it never occurred to them to recognize the bay.

On the Point of Pines they erected a large wooden cross, and carved on it the words: " Dig at the foot of this and you will find a writing."

According to Crespi this is what was written:

"The overland expedition which left San Diego on the 14th of July, 1769, under the command of Don Gaspar de Portolá, Governor of California, reached the channel of Santa Barbara on the 9th of August, and passed Point Concepcion on the 27th of the same month. It arrived at the Sierra de Santa Lucía on the 13th of September; entered that range of mountains on the 17th of the same month, and emerged from it on the 1st of October; on the same day caught sight of Point Pinos, and the harbors on its north and south sides, without discoving any indications or landmarks of the Bay of Monterey. We determined to push on farther in search of it, and on the 30th of October got sight of Point Reyes and the Farallones, at the Bay of San Francisco, which are seven in number. The expedition strove to reach Point Reyes, but was hindered by an immense arm of the sea, which, extending to a great distance inland, compelled them to make an enormous circuit for that purpose. In consequence of this and other difficulties — the greatest of all being the absolute want of food,— the expedition was compelled to turn back, believing that they must have passed the harbor of Monterey without discovering it. We started on return

from the Bay of San Francisco on the 11th of November; passed Point Año Nuevo on the 19th, and
reached this point and harbor of Pinos on the 27th
of the same month. From that date until the present 9th of December, we have used every effort to
find the Bay of Monterey, searching the coast, not-
withstanding its ruggedness, far and wide, but in
vain. At last, undeceived and despairing of finding
it, after so many efforts, sufferings, and labors, and
having left of all our provisions but fourteen small
sacks of flour, we leave this place to-day for San
Diego. I beg of Almighty God to guide us; and for
you, traveler, who may read this, that He may
guide you also, to the harbor of eternal salvation.

"Done, in this harbor of Pinos, the 9th of December, 1769.

"If the commanders of the schooners, either the
San José or the Principe, should reach this place
within a few days after this date, on learning the
accounts of this writing, and of the distressed condition of this expedition, we beseech them to follow
the coast down closely toward San Diego, so that if
we should be happy enough to catch sight of them,
we may be able to apprize them by signals, flags,
and firearms of the place where help and provisions may reach us."

The next day the whole party started back to
San Diego, making the journey fairly well, in spite
of illness and lack of proper food. Though dis-

appointed at Portolá's failure, Serra had no idea
of abandoning his project of founding a mission at
Monterey. He made further preparations, and in
about three months after Portolá's return a newly
organized expedition left San Diego. It consisted
of two divisions, one by land, again commanded
by Portolá, and one by sea. This time the good
Father wisely chose for himself to go by sea, and
embarked on the San Antonio, which was the only
ship he had in sailing condition. In about a
month Portolá's land party reached the Point of
Pines, and there they found their cross still standing. According to Laura Bride Powers, " great
festoons of abalone-shells hung around its arms,
with strings of fish and meat; feathers projected
from the top, and bundles of arrows and sticks lay
at its base. All this was to appease the stranger
gods, and the Indians told them that at nightfall
the terrible cross would stretch its white arms into
space, and grow skyward higher and higher, till it
would touch the stars, then it would burst into a
blaze and glow throughout the night."

Suddenly, as they came back through the forest
from the Point of Pines, the thought came both to
Crespi and Portolá that here, after all, was the lost
bay of Vizcaino. In this thought they ran over

the landmarks of his description, and found all of them, though the harbor was less important than Vizcaino had believed. Since that day no one has doubted the existence of the Bay of Monterey.

A week later, the San Antonio arrived, coming in sight around the Point of Pines, and was guided to its anchorage by bonfires along the beach. The party landed at the mouth of the little brook which flows down a rocky bank to the sea. On the 3rd of June, 1770, Father Serra and his associates " took possession of the land in the name of the King of Spain, hoisting the Spanish flag, pulling out some of the grass and throwing stones here and there, making formal entry of the proceedings." On the same day Serra began his mission by erecting a cross, hanging bells from a tree, and saying mass under the venerable oak where the Carmelite friars accompanying Vizcaino celebrated it in 1602. Around this landing grew up the town of Monterey.

At a point just back from the shore, near the old live-oak tree under which the Padre rendered thanks, there has long stood a commemorative cross. On the hill above where the Padre stood looking out over the beautiful bay, there was placed one hundred and twenty years later, by the kind interest of a good woman, a noble statue, in gray granite, representing Father Serra as he stepped from his boat.

A fortress, or *presidio*, was built, and Monterey was made the capital of Alta California. But the mission was not located at the town. It was placed five miles farther south, where there were better pasturage and shelter. This was on a beautiful slope of the hill, flanked by a fertile valley opening out to the glittering sea, with the mountains of Santa Lucía in front and a great pine forest behind. The valley was named Carmelo, in honor of Vizcaino's Carmelite friars, and the mission was named for San Carlos Borromeo.

The present church of Monterey was not a mission church, but the chapel of the *presidio*, or barracks. It is now, according to Father Casanova, the oldest building in California. The old Mission of San Diego, first founded of all, was burned by the Indians. It was afterwards rebuilt, but this took place after the chapel in Monterey was finished. The mission in Carmelo was not completed until later, as the Padre was obliged to secure authority from Mexico, that he might place it on the pasture lands of Carmelo, instead of the sand-hills of Monterey.

When the discoveries of Portolá and Ortega had been reported at San Diego, the shores of this inland

sea of San Francisco seemed a most favorable station for another mission.   Among the missions
already dedicated to the saints, none had yet been
found for the great father of the Franciscan order,
St. Francis of Assisi, the beloved saint who could call
the birds and who knew the speech of all animals.
Before this, Father Serra had said to Governor
Galvez, "And for our Father St. Francis is there to
be no mission?"   And Galvez answered, " If St.
Francis wants a mission, let him show his port, and
we will found the mission there."

And now the lost port of St. Francis was found,
and it was the most beautiful of all, with the noblest
of harbors, and the fairest of views toward the hills
and the sea.   So the new mission was called for
him, the Mission San Francisco de los Dolores.
For the Creek Dolores, the " brook of sorrows,"
flowed by the mission, and gave it part of its name.
But Dolores stream is long since obliterated, forming part of the sewage system of San Francisco.*

Thus was founded

"that wondrous city, now apostate to the creed,
O'er whose youthful walls the Padre saw the angel's golden
  reed."

_____

* The limits of San Francisco Bay, as now understood, were ascer-
tained at the time of the founding of the mission, and the name was
then formally adopted.

Meanwhile, following San Diego de Alcalá and San Carlos Borromeo, a long series of missions was established, each one bearing the sonorous Spanish name of some saint or archangel, each in some beautiful sunny valley, half-hidden by oaks, and each a day's ride distant from the next. In the most charming nook of the Santa Lucía Mountains was built San Antonio de Pádua; in the finest open pastures of the Coast Range, San Luis Obispo de Tolosa. In the rich valley, above the city of the Queen of the Angels, the beautiful church of San Gabriel Arcángel was dedicated to the leader of the hosts of heaven. Later, came the magnificent San Juan Capistrano, ruined by earthquakes in 1812. In its garden still stands the largest pepper-tree in Southern California.

Then Santa Clara was built in the center of the fairest valley of the State. Next came San Buenaventura and Santa Barbara, for the coast Indians of the south, and Santa Cruz, for those to the north of Monterey Bay. In the Salinas Valley, along the "*Camino real*," or royal highway, from the south to the north, were built Nuestra Señora de la Soledad and San Miguel Arcángel. A day's journey from Carmelo, in the valley of the Pájaro, arose San Juan Bautista. In the charming valley of

Santa Ynez, still hidden from the tourist, a day's journey apart, were Santa Ynez and La Purisima Concepcion.   East of the Bay of San Francisco, in a nook famous for vineyards, arose the Mission San José.

In the broad, rocky pastures above Los Angeles, arose San Fernando Rey de España, while midway between San Diego and San Juan Capistrano was placed the stateliest of all the missions, dedicated, with its rich river valley, to the memory of San Luis Rey de Fráncia.   Finally, to the north of San Francisco Bay, was built San Rafael, small, but charmingly situated, and then San Francisco Solano, still farther on in Sonoma. This, the northernmost outpost of the saints, the last, weakest, and smallest, was first to die.   It was founded in 1823, fifty years after the Mission San Diego.

Wherever you find in California a warm, sunny valley leading from the ocean back to the purple mountains, with a clear stream in its midst, and filled in summer with blue haze, around it steep slopes on which grapes may grow, you have found a mission valley, and these grapes are mission grapes.   Somewhere in it you will see a cluster of large, wide-spreading pepper-trees, with delicate light-green foliage, or a grove of gnarled olives,

MISSION OF SAN ANTONIO DE PADUA.

looking like stunted willows, or, perhaps, a cluster
of old pear-trees, or sometimes a tall palm. Near
these you will find the ruins of old houses of
adobe, wherein once dwelt the Indian neophytes.
These houses are clustered around the walls, now
almost in ruins, of the mission itself, which had
its chapel, refectory, and baptistry, and in all its
details it resembled closely a parish church of Italy
or Spain.

The mission was usually laid out in the form of
a hollow square, inclosed by a wall of adobe, twelve
feet high, the whole inclosure being two or three
hundred feet square. In the center of this square was
a chapel, also of adobe; for the sun of California is
kind to California's children, and a house of dried
mud will withstand the scanty rains of a century.
Some of these old chapels are still used, but the
roofs of most of them have long since fallen in, and
the ornaments have been removed to decorate some
other building. The mission churches were built
like mimic cathedrals, cathedrals of mud instead of
marble, and, like their great models, each had its
altar, with candles and crucifix, its vessels of holy
water, and on the walls the inevitable paintings of
heaven and purgatory. Their most charming feature was the arched cloister, a feature which has

been retained and beautified in the architecture of Leland Stanford Jr. University, at Palo Alto.

Each church, too, had its little chime of bells, some of which were partly of gold or silver, as well as of brass. During the early enthusiasm, when the mission bells were cast, old heirlooms from Spain, rings, vases, and ancestral goblets from which had been " drunk the red wine of Tarragon," were thrown into the molten metal. And when these consecrated bells chimed out the Angelus at the sunset hour, with the sound of their voices all evil spirits were driven away, and no harm could come to man or beast or growing grain.

> " Bells of the past, whose long-forgotten music
>   Still fills the wide expanse,
>   Tingeing the sober twilight of the present
>   With color of romance ;
>
>   I hear you call, and see the sun descending
>   On rock and wave and sand,
>   As down the coast the mission voices blending,
>   Girdle the heathen land.
>
> " Within the circle of your incantation
>   No blight nor mildew falls,
>   Nor fierce unrest nor sordid low ambition
>   Passes those airy walls.
>
>   Borne on the swell of your long waves receding
>   I touch the farther past.
>   I see the dying glow of Spanish glory,
>   The sunset dream and last.

.   .   .   .

"Your voices break and falter in the darkness,
  Break, falter, and are still,
And veiled and mystic, like the Host descending,
  The sun sinks from the hill."*

Around the church were built storehouses, work-shops, granaries, barracks for the soldiers, — in short, everything necessary for comfort and security. Each mission was at once fortress, refuge, church, and town. The little town grew in time more and more to resemble its fellows in old Spain. Bull-fights and other festivals were held in the *plaza*, or public square, in front of the *presidio*, or governor's house, and the long, low, whitewashed *hacienda*, or tavern.

About the mission arose a great farm. Vines and olives were planted, and often long avenues of shade-trees. The level lands were sown to barley and oats; great herds of cattle and horses roamed over the hills. The sale of wine, and especially of hides, brought in each year an increasing revenue. The poor, struggling missions became rich. The commanders kept up a dignity worthy of the representatives of the Spanish king, though often they had little enough to command. It is said that one of them, wishing to fire a salute in honor of some foreign vessel, first sent on board to borrow powder.

*Bret Harte.

In the words of Bret Harte, with the *comandante* the days "slipped by in a delicious monotony of simple duties, unbroken by incident or interruption. The regularly recurring feasts and saint's days, the half-yearly courier from San Diego, the rare transport ship, and rarer foreign vessels, were the mere details of his patriarchal life. If there was no achievement, there was certainly no failure. Abundant harvests and patient industry amply supplied the wants of the *presidio* and mission. Isolated from the family of nations, the wars which shook the world concerned them not so much as the last earthquake; the struggle that emancipated their sister colonies on the other side of the continent had to them no suggestiveness. It was that glorious Indian summer of California history, that bland, indolent autumn of Spanish rule, so soon to be followed by the wintry storms of Mexican independence and the reviving spring of American conquest."

The Indians were usually gathered about the mission by force or by persuasion. Being baptized with holy water, they were taught to build houses, raise grain, and take care of cattle. In place of their savage rites, they learned to count their beads and say their prayers. They learned also to work,

MISSION OF SAN ANTONIO DE PADUA. INTERIOR OF CHAPEL.

and were pious and generally contented. But these California Indians, at the best, were far inferior to those of the East. " When attached to the mission," Mr. Soulé says, " they were an industrious, contented, and numerous class, though, indeed, in intelligence and manly spirit they were little better than the beasts, after all."

The Jesuit Father, Venegas, remarks, discouragingly : "It is not easy for Europeans who were never out of their own country to conceive an adequate idea of these people. Even in the least frequented quarters of the globe there is not a nation so stupid, of such contracted ideas, and weak, both in body and in mind, as the unhappy Californians. Their characteristics are stupidity and insensibility, want of knowledge and reflection, inconstancy, impetuosity, and blindness of appetite, excessive sloth, abhorrence of all fatigue of every kind, however trifling or brutal,— in fine, a most wretched want of everything which constitutes the real man and makes him rational, inventive, tractable, and useful to himself and others." All of which goes to show that climate is not everything, and that contact with other minds and other people, with the sifting that rigorous conditions enforce, may outweigh all the advantages of the fairest climate. The highest development comes with the fewest barriers to migration, to competition, and to the spread of ideas.

The destruction of the missions and the advent of our Anglo-Saxon freedom has been for the Indian and his kind only loss and wrong. He has become an alien and tramp, with his half-brother, the despised Greaser.

The mission fathers left no place for idleness on the part of their converts, or "neophytes"; nor did they make much provision for the development of the individual. The Indians were to work, and to work hard and steadily, for the glory of the church and the prosperity of the nation. In return they were insured from all harm in this world and in the world to come. The rule of the Padre was often severe, sometimes cruel, but not demoralizing, and the Indians reached a higher grade of industry and civilization than the same race has attained otherwise before or since.

Believing that the use of the rod was necessary to the Indians' salvation, the Padres were in no danger of sparing it, and thus spoiling their children. The good Father Serra would as "soon have doubted his right to breathe as his right to flog the Indian converts"; and meek and quiet though these converts usually were, there were not wanting times when they turned about in sullen resistance. The annals of some of the missions show a series of events that may well have discouraged the most enthusiastic of missionaries. The unconverted Indians, or "gentiles," of Southern California were heathens indeed, and they made repeated attacks upon the missions by day, or stole their stock or burned their houses by night. Volleys of arrows not unfrequently greeted the priests on their return from morning mass.

In San Diego, faith in the power of gunpowder to hurt long preceded any belief in the power of the cross to save. For a whole year after the mission was founded, not a convert was made. The sole San Diego Indian in Father Serra's service was a hired interpreter, who did not have a particle of reverence for his employer's work. "In all these missionary annals of the Northwest," says Bancroft, "there is no other instance where paganism remained so long stubborn as in San Diego."

And the converts made at such cost of threats and promises were always ready to backslide. It was hard to convert any unless they subjugated all. The influence of the many outside would often stampede the few within the fold.

In one of the numerous uprisings at San Diego the Fathers were victorious over the Indians; the warriors were flogged, and thus converted, and their four chiefs were condemned to death. The sentence of death, according to Bancroft, read as follows:

"Deeming it useful to the service of God, the king, and the public good, I sentence them to a violent death by musket shots, on the 11th of April, at 9 A.M., the troops to be present at the execution, under arms; and also all the Christian rancherias subject to the San Diego Mission, that they may be warned to act righteously."

To the priests who were to assist at the last sacrament, the following grim directions was given:

"You will co-operate for the good of their souls, in the understanding that if they do not accept the salutary waters of holy baptism, they die on Saturday morning; and if they do accept, they die all the same."

The character of the first great mission chief, Junípero Serra, is thus summed up by Bancroft:

"All his energy and enthusiasm were directed to the performance of his missionary duties as outlined in the regulations of his order and the instruction of his superiors. Limping from mission to mission, with a lame foot that must never be cured, fasting much and passing sleepless nights, depriving himself of comfortable clothing and nutritious food, he felt that he was imitating the saints and martyrs who were the ideals of his sickly boyhood, and in recompense of abstinence he was happy. He was kind-hearted and charitable to all, but most strict in his enforcement of religious duties. It never occurred to him to doubt his absolute right to flog his neophytes for any slight negligence in matters of the faith. His holy desires trembled within him like earthquake throbs. In his eyes there was but one object worth living for — the performance of religious duty; and but one way to accomplish that object — a strict and literal compliance with Franciscan rules. He could never understand that there was anything beyond the narrow field of his vision. He could apply religious enthusiasm to practical affairs. Because he was a grand missionary, he was none the less a money-maker and civilizer; but money-making and civilizing were adjuncts only to mission work, and all not for his glory, but for the glory of God."

After Junípero Serra came a saner and wiser, if not a better, man, the Padre Fermin Lasuen. I need not go into details in regard to him or his life. No miracles followed his path, and no saint made him the object of spectacular intervention; but his gentle earnestness counted for more in the

development of Old California than that of any
other man.   Of Lasuen, Bancroft says:

"In him were united the qualities that make up
the ideal Padre, without taint of hypocrisy or cant.
He was a frank, kind-hearted old man, who made
friends of all he met. Of his fervent piety there
are abundant proofs, and his piety and humility
were of an agreeable type, unobtrusive, and blended
with common sense. He overcame obstacles in the
way of duty, but he created no obstacles for the
mere sake of surmounting them. He was not a
man to limp through life on a sore leg if a cure
could be found. . . . First among the Califor-
nian prelates let us ever rank Fermin de Lasuen, as
a friar who rose above his environment and lived
many years in advance of his times."

Thirteen years after the serene founding of the
Mission San Francisco came the first shock to the
community, thus noticed in a letter from the governor of the territory to the *comandante* at San
Francisco:

" Whenever there may arrive at the Port of San
Francisco a ship named the Columbia, said to
belong to General Washington, of the American
States, commanded by John Kendrick, which sailed
from Boston in September, 1787, bound on a voyage
of discovery to the Russian establishments on the
northern coast of this peninsula, you will cause the

said vessel to be examined with caution and delicacy, using for this purpose a small boat which you
have in your possession."

Afterwards another enemy, almost as dangerous
as the Yankee, appeared in the shape of Russians
from Alaska. They brought down a colony of
Kodiak Indians, or Aleuts, and established themselves at Fort Ross, north of San Francisco. The
Spaniards then founded the missions of San Rafael
and Solano in front of the Russians, to head them
off, as the priest makes the sign of the cross to ward
off Satan. Trading with the Russians was forbidden, but, nevertheless, the Russian vessels, on one
pretext or another, made repeated visits to the Bay
of San Francisco. The Spaniards had no boats in
the bay, and could not prevent the ingress of the
Russian and American traders. One of the singu-
lar facts in connection with the missions is that the
Padres made no use of the sea, and the missions
usually kept no boats at all, and so the Spanish
officials were forced to receive in friendliness many
encroachments which they were powerless to prevent.

In 1842, as the seals grew scarce around Bodegas
Head, the Russians, to the great satisfaction of the
Spaniards, disappeared as suddenly as they came.

The joy of the missions was short-lived, for seven years later gold was discovered, California was ceded to the United States, and the most remarkable invasion known in history followed. Over the mountains, across the plains, by the Isthmus, and by the Horn they came, that wonderful procession which Bret Harte has made so familiar to us — Truthful James, Tennessee's Partner, Jack Hamlin, John Oakhurst, Flynn of Virginia, Abner Dean of Angels, Brown of Calaveras, Yuba Bill, Sandy McGee, the Scheezicks, the Man of No Account, and all the rest. And the California of the gambler and the gold-seeker succeeds the California of the Padre.

Numerous causes had meanwhile contributed to the decline of the Spanish missions. They had been supported at first by a Pious Fund, obtained by subscriptions in Mexico and Spain. After the separation of these two countries, this fund was lost, its interest being regularly embezzled by Mexican officials, and, finally, the principal, it is said, was taken in one lump by the President, Santa Ana. Still the missions were able to hold their own until the Mexican Government removed the Indians from the control of the Padres, for the benefit, I suppose, of the "Indian ring." The secular control of the native tribes was, in Mexican hands, an utter failure. The Indians, now no longer compelled to work, no longer well fed and comfortably clothed, were scattered about the country as paupers and tramps. The missions, after repeated interferences of this sort, fell into a rapid decline, and at the time that California was ceded to the United States, not one of them was in successful operation. A few of the churches are still partly occupied, as at San Luis Obispo, San Capistrano, and San Miguel. The Mission of Santa Barbara is still intact, and has yet its little bands of monks. A few, like San Carlos, have been partially saved or partially restored, thanks to the loving interest of Father Casanova and others; but the Indians are gone, and neither wealth nor influence remains with the missions. Most of them are crumbling ruins, and have already taken their place as curiosities and relics of the past. Some of them, as the noble San Antonio de Pádua and the stately San Luis Rey, are exquisitely beautiful, even in ruins. Of others, as San Rafael, not a trace remains, and its spot can be kept green only in memory. It is said that at San Antonio, a mission once numbering fourteen hundred souls, and rearing the finest horses in California, the last priest lived all alone for years, and supported himself by raising geese and selling the tiles from the mission roof. When he died, ten years ago, no one was left to care for his beloved mission, which is rapidly falling into utter decay.

So faded away the California of the Padre, and left no stain on the pages of our history.

MISSION OF SAN ANTONIO DE PADUA — SIDE OF THE CHAPEL, WITH THE OLD PEAR-TREES.

THE CONQUEST OF JUPITER PEN.

IN a cleft of the high Alps stands the Hospice of the Great Saint Bernard. Its tall, cold, stone buildings are half-buried in ice in the winter, while even in summer the winds, dense with snow, shriek and howl as they make their way through the notch in the mountain. Its little lake, cold and dark, frozen solid in winter, is covered with cakes of floating ice under the sky of July. The scanty grass around it forms a thick, low turf, which is studded with bodiless blue gentians, primroses, and other Alpine flowers. Overhanging the lake are the frost-bitten crags of the Mountain of Death; and the other mountains about, though less dismally named, are not more cheerful to the traveler. Along the lake margin winds the narrow bridle-path, which follows rushing rivulets in zigzags down steep flower-carpeted slopes to the pine woods of Saint Rémy, far below. Among the pines the path widens to a wagon-road, whence it descends through green pastures, purple with autumnal crocus, past beggarly villages, whose houses crowd together, like fright-

ened cattle in a herd, through beech woods, vineyards, and grain-fields, till at last it comes to its
rest amid the high stone walls of the old city of
Aosta, named for Augustus Cæsar. Above Aosta
are the sources of the river Po, one of the chief of
these being the Dora Baltea, in a deep gorge half-hid
by chestnut-trees. It is twenty miles from the lake
to the river — twenty miles of wild mountain in-
cline — twenty miles from Switzerland to Italy,
from the eternal snows and faint-colored flowers of
the frigid zone, to the dust, and glare of the torrid.

The Hospice of the Great Saint Bernard stands
thus in a narrow mountain notch, with only room
for itself and its lake, while above it, on either
side, are jagged heights dashed with snow-banks,
their summits frosted with eternal ice.

It is a large stone building, three stories high,
beside the two attic floors of the steep, sloping roof.
A great square house of cold, gray stone, as unat-
tractive as a barn or a woolen-mill, plain, cold, and
solid. At one end of the main building is a stone
addition precisely like the building itself. On the
other side of the bridle-path is an outbuilding — a
tall stone shed, "the Hotel of Saint Louis," three
stories high, as plain and uncompromising as the
Hospice is. The front door of the main building

THE GREAT SAINT BERNARD.

is on the side away from the lake. From this
door down the north side of the mountain the path
descends steeply from the crest of the Pennine Alps
to the valley of the Rhone, even more swiftly than
the path on the south side drops downward to the
valley of the Po.

As one approaches the Hospice he is met by a
noisy band of great dogs, yellow and white, with
the loudest of bass voices, barking incessantly, eager
to pull you out of the snow, and finding that you
do not need this sort of rescue, apparently equally
eager to tear you to pieces for having deceived
them. Classical names these dogs still bear — names
worthy of the mountain long sacred to Jupiter, on
which the Hospice is built — Jupitère, Junon, Mars,
Vulcan, Pluton, the inevitable Léon, and the in-
domitable Turc, and all have for the traveler such
a greeting as only a band of big, idle dogs can give.
These dogs are not so large nor so well kept as the
Saint Bernard dogs we see in American cities, but
they have the same great head, huge feet and legs,
and the same intelligent eye, as if they were capable of doing anything if they would only stop barking long enough to think of something else.

The inside of the house corresponds to its outer
appearance. Thick, heavy triple doors admit you

to a cold hall floored with stone. Adjoining this is a parlor, likewise floored with the coldest of stone, and this parlor is used as the dining-room and waiting-room for travelers. Its walls are hung with pictures, many of them valuable works of art, the gifts of former guests, while its chilly air is scantily warmed by a small fireplace, on which whoever will may throw pine boughs and fragments of the spongy wood of the fir. By this fire the guests take their turn in getting partly warmed, then pass away to shiver in the outer wastes of the room.

In this room the travelers are served with plain repasts, princes and peasants alike, coarse bread, red wine, coffee, and boiled meat; everything about the table neat and clean, but with no pretense at pampering the appetite. You take whatever you please without money and without price. Should you care to pay your way, or care to help on the work of the Hospice, you can leave your mite, be it large or small, in a box near the door of the chapel. The guest-rooms are plain but comfortable — a few religious pictures on the walls; tall, old-fashioned beasteads, with abundant feather-beds and warm blankets. For one night only all persons who come are welcome. The next day all alike, unless sick or crippled, must pass on.

HOSPICE OF THE GREAT SAINT BERNARD.

There are about a dozen monks in the Hospice now, all of them young men, devoted to their work, and some of them at least intelligent and generously educated. The hard climate and the exposure of winter breaks down their health before they are old. When they become unable to carry on the duties of the Hospice, they are sent down the mountains to Martigny, while others come up to take their places. There are beautiful days in the summer-time, but no season of the year is free from severity. Even in July and August the ground is half the time white with snow. Terrible blasts sweep through the mountains; for the commonest summer shower in the valleys below is, in these heights, a raging snow-storm, and its snow-laden winds are never faced with impunity.

We visited the Hospice in July, 1890. We drove from Aosta up to Saint Rémy, a little village crowded in on the side of the mountain, where the pine-trees cease. The light rain which followed us out from Saint Rémy changed to snow as we came up the rocky slopes. By the time we reached the Hospice it became a blinding sleet. The ground was only whitened, so that the dogs who came barking to meet us had no need to dig us out from the drifts. In this they seemed disappointed, and barked again.

Once inside the walls, one cared not to go out. Many travelers came up the mountain that day. Among them were a man and his wife, Italian peasants, who had been over the mountains to spend a day or two with friends in some village on the Swiss side, and were now returning home. Man and woman were dressed in their peasants' best, and with them was a little girl, some four years old. The child carried a toy horse in her hands, the gift of some friend below. As they toiled up the steep path in the blinding snow, all of them thinly clad and dressed only for summer, they seemed chilled through and through, while the child was almost frozen. The monks came out to meet them, took the child in their arms, and brought her and her parents to the fire, covered her shoulders with a warm shawl, and, after feeding them, sent them down the mountain to their home in the valley, warmed and filled. This was a simple act, the easiest of all their many duties, but it was a very touching one. Such duties make up the simple round of their lives.

In the storms of winter the work of the Hospice takes a sterner cast. From November to May the gales are incessant. The snow piles up in billows, and in the whirling clouds all traces of human oc-

cupation are obliterated. There are many peasants and workingmen who go forth from Italy into Switzerland and France, and who wish to return home when their summer labors are over. To these the pass of the Great Saint Bernard is the only route which they can afford. The long railway rides and the great distances of the Simplon and the Saint Gotthard would mean the using up of their scanty earnings. If they go home at all, they must trust their lives to the storms and the monks, and take the path which leads by the Hospice. So they come over day after day, the winter long. No matter how great the storm, the dogs are on the watch. In the last winter, of the many who came, not one was lost.

This is the Hospice as it stands to-day. I come next to tell its story and the story of its founder. I tell it, in the most part, from a little volume in French, which some modest and nameless monk of the Hospice has compiled from the old Latin records of the monks who have gone before him. This volume he has printed, as he says, " for the use of the faithful in the parishes which lie next the Alps, and which, in his time, the good Saint Bernard* passed through." This story I must tell

---

*St. Bernard de Menthon must not be confounded with Bernard de Clairvaux, born in 1091, the preacher of the Crusades.

in his own spirit, in some degree at least, else I should have no right to tell it at all.

In the tenth century, he informs us, the dark ages of Europe could scarcely have been darker. Weak and wicked kings, the dregs of the worn-out blood of Charlemagne, misruled France, while along the northern coast the Normans robbed and plundered at their will. Even the church had her share of crimes and scandals. In this dark time, says the chronicle, " God, who had promised to be with His own to the end of the centuries, did not fail to raise up in that darkness great saints who should teach the people to lift their eyes toward heaven; to rise above afflictions; not to take the form of the world for a permanent habitation, and to suffer its pains with patience, in the prospect of eternity."

It happened that in the days of King Raoul, in the Castle of Menthon, on the north bank of the lake of Annécy, in Savoy, in the year 923, Bernard de Menthon was born. His father was the Baron Richard, famous among the noblemen of the time, while his mother, the Lady Bernoline, was illustrious for virtues. The young Bernard was a fair child, and his history, as seen from the perspective of his monkish historian, shows that even in his

JUTIÈRE.

earliest youth he was predestined for saintship. Even before he could walk, the little child would join his hands in the attitude of supplication, and murmur words which might have been prayers. While still very young, he brought in a book one day and asked his mother to teach him to read, and when she would not, or could not, he wept, for the books in which even then he delighted were the prayer-books of the church.

He grew up bright and beautiful, and his father was proud of him, and determined that he should take his part in public life. But Bernard's thoughts ran in other channels. He spent his moments in copying psalms, and in writing down the words of divine service which he heard. Even in his seventh year he began to practice austerities and self-castigation, which he kept up through his life. He chose for his model Saint Nicholas, the saint who through the ages has been kind to children. Him he resolved to imitate, and to walk always in his steps.

The University of Paris had been founded by Charlemagne more than a century before, and this university was then the Mecca of all ambitious youth. To the University of Paris his father decided to send him. But his mother feared the influence of the gay capital, and wished to keep Bernard by her side. But the boy said, "Virtue has too deep a root in my heart, mother, for the air of Paris to tarnish it. I will bring back more of science, but not less of purity." And to Paris he went. Here he studied law, to please his father, and theology, to please himself. "As Tobias lived faithful in Nineveh," so the chronicle says, "thus lived Bernard in Paris." In the midst of snares unnumbered, he only redoubled his austerities — *"in sanctitate persistens, studiosus valde,"* so the record says.

His thoughts ran on the misery of humanity, which he measured by the abasement to which Christ had submitted in order to effect its redemption. A great influence in his life came from Germain, his tutor, a man who had lived the life of a scholar in the world, and who had at last withdrawn to sanctity and prayer. Although Bernard knew that his father expected a brilliant future for him, and that he hoped to effect for him a marriage in some family of the great of those days, yet he took upon himself the vow of celibacy. "God lives in virgin souls," he said. There is a record of an argument with Germain, in which his tutor tries to test the strength of his purpose. Ger-

MONKS OF THE GREAT SAINT BERNARD.

main tells him that even in a monastery evil cannot be excluded, and that many even of the most
austere monks live lives of petty jealousy and
ignoble ambition. "There are many," Germain
says, "who are saved in the struggle of the world
who would be shipwrecked in a monastery." But
Bernard is steadfast in his choice. "Happy are
those who have chosen to dwell in God's court,
and to sleep on His estate." Thus day and night
he struggles against all temptations of worldly
glory or pleasure.

Then his father calls him home; and when he
has returned to Annécy, Bernard finds that every
preparation has been made for his approaching
wedding with the daughter of the great Lord of
Miolans. "*Sponsa pulchra*," beautiful bride, this
young woman was, according to the record, and
doubtless this was true. The attitude of Bernard
toward this marriage his father and mother could
not understand. He held back constantly, and
urged all sorts of objections to its immediate con-
summation, but on no ground which seemed to
them reasonable. So the wedding-day was set.
The house was full of guests. Every gate and door
of the castle was crowded by armed retainers, and
there seemed to be no escape. Bernard retired to

his own room, and in the oldest manuscripts are given the words of his prayer:

" My adorable Creator, Thou who with thy celestial light enlightened those who invoke with faith and confidence, and Thou my Jesus, Divine Redeemer of men and Saviour of souls, lend a favorable ear to my humble prayer; spread on thy servant the treasures of your infinite mercy. I know that Thou never abandonest those who place in you their hope; deliver me, I supplicate Thee, from the snares which the world have offered me. Break these nets in which the world tries to take me; permit not that the enemy prevail over thy servant, that adulation may enfeeble my heart. I abandon myself entirely to Thee. I throw myself into the arms of thy infinite mercy, hoping that Thou wilt save me, and wilt reject not my demand."

Then to the good Saint Nicholas:

"Amiable shepherd, faithful guide, holy priest, thou who art my protector and my refuge, together with God, and His holy mother, the happy Virgin Mary, obtain me, I pray thee, by thy merits, the grace of triumph over the obstacles the world opposes to my vow of consecrating myself to God without reserve — in return for the property, the pleasures, and honors here below, of which I abandon my part, obtain me spiritual good all the course of my life, and eternal happiness after my death."

Then Bernard retired to sleep, and in a dream Saint Nicholas stood before him and uttered these words:

"Bernard, servant of God the Lord, who never betrays those who put their confidence in Him, calls thee to follow Him. An immortal crown is reserved for thee. Leave at once thy father's house and go to Aosta. There in the cathedral thou shalt meet an old man called Pièrre. He will welcome thee; thou shalt live with him, and he shall teach thee the road thou should traverse. For my part, I shall be thy protector, and will not for an instant abandon thee."

Then Bernard opened his eyes and the vision had disappeared. He was overcome with joy. His resolution was taken. Though he knew no way out of the castle, nor from the bedroom in the tower, in which he had been locked by his thoughtful father, yet he was ready to go.

Taking up a pen, he wrote to his father this letter:

"Very dear parents, rejoice with me that the Lord calls me to His service. I follow Him to arrive sooner at the port of salvation, the sole object of my vows. Do not worry about me, nor take the trouble to seek me. I renounce the marriage, which was ever against my will. I renounce all that concerns the world. All my desires turn

toward heaven, whither I would arrive. I take the
road this minute.   BERNARD DE MENTHON."

Laying the letter on the table, he soon found
himself on the way outside the castle grounds, and
along this path he hurried, over the mountain
passes, toward the city of Aosta. So say the oldest
manuscripts; but in the later stories the details are
more fully described. From these it would appear
that Bernard leaped from the window eighteen or
twenty feet, his naked feet striking on a bare rock.
On he ran through the night; on over dark and
lonely paths in a country still uninhabited; over
the stony fields and wild watercourses of the
Graian Alps, and when the morning dawned he
found himself in the city of Aosta, a hundred
miles from Annécy.

In an old painting the manner of his escape is
shown in detail. As he drops from the window he
is supported by Saint Nicholas on the one side, and
an angel on the other, and underneath the painting
is the legend *" Emporté par Miracle."* It is said,
too, that in former times the prints of his hands
on the stone window-sill, and of his naked feet on
the rock below, were both plainly visible. Eight
hundred years later the good Father Pièrre Verre
celebrated mass in the old room in which Bernard

was confined; and he reports at that time there was both on the window-sill and on the rock below only the merest trace of the imprints left by Bernard. One could not then "even be sure that they were made by hand or foot." But the chronicle wisely says: "Time, in effacing these marks and rendering them doubtful, has never effaced the tradition of the fact among the people of Annécy."

In the morning, consternation reigned within the castle. The Lord of Menthon was filled with disgust, shame, and confusion. The Lord of Miolans thought that he and his daughter were the victims of a trick, and he would take no explanation or excuse. Only the sword might efface the stain upon his honor. The marriage feast would have ended in a scene of blood were it not, according to the chronicle, that "God, always admirable in His saints," sent as an angel of peace the very person who had been most cruelly wronged. The Lady of Miolans, "*sponsa pulchra*" beyond a doubt, took up the cause of her delinquent bridegroom, whom God had called, she said, to take some nobler part. When peace had been made, she followed his example, taking the veil in a neighboring convent, where, after many years of virtuous living, she died, full of days and full of merits. "*Sponsa ipsius,*" so the record says, " *in qua sancte et religiose dies suos clausit*"; a bride who in sanctity and religious days closed her life.

Meanwhile, beyond the Graian Alps and beyond the reach of his father's information, Bernard was safe. In Aosta he was kindly received by Pièrre, the Archdeacon. He entered into the service of the church, and there, in spite of his humility and his self-abasement, he won the favor of all with whom he had to deal. "God wills," the chronicle says, "that His ministers should shine by their sanctity and their science." "Saint Paul commends prudence, gravity, modesty, unselfishness, and hospitality," and to these precepts Bernard was ever faithful. He lived in the simplest way, like a hermit in his personal relations, but never out of the life of the world. He was not a man eager to save his own soul only, but the bodies and souls of his neighbors. He dressed in the plainest garb. He drank from a rude wooden cup. Wine he never touched, and water but rarely. The juice of bitter herbs was his beverage, and by every means possible he strove to reduce his body to servitude. When he came, years later, to his deathbed, it was his sole regret that it was a *bed* where he was to die, instead of the bare boards on which he was wont to sleep.

His fame as a preacher spread far and wide. There are many traditions of his eloquence, and the memory of his words was fondly cherished wherever his sweet, rich voice was heard. "From the mountains of Savoy to Milan and Turin, and even to the Lake of Geneva," says the chronicle, "his memory was dear." So, in due time, after the death of Pièrre, Bernard was made Archdeacon of Aosta.

In these times the high Alps were filled with Saracen brigands and other heathen freebooters, who celebrated in the mountain fastnesses their monstrous rites. In the mountains above Aosta the god Pen had long been worshiped; the word *pen* in Celtic meaning the highest. Later, Julius Cæsar conquered these wild tribes, and imposed upon them the religion of the Roman Empire. A statue of Jupiter ("*Jove optimo maximo*") was set up in the mountain in the place of the idol Pen. Afterwards, by way of compromise, the Romans permitted the two to become one, and the people worshiped Jovis Pennius (Jupiter Pen), the great god of the highest mountains. A statue of Jupiter Pen was set up by the side of the lake in the great pass of the mountain; and from Jupiter Pen these mountains took the name of Pennine Alps, which they bear to this day. The pass itself was called Mons Jovis, the Mountain of Jove, and this, in due time, became shortened to Mont Joux. Through this pass of Mont Joux the armies of every nation have marched, the heroes of every age, from Saint Peter, who, the legend says, came over in the year 57, down to Napoleon, who passed nearly eighteen centuries later, on a much less worthy errand. The Hotel " Déjeuner de Napoléon," in the little village of " Bourg Saint Pièrre," recalls in its name the story of both these visits.

In the earliest days a refuge hut was built by the side of the statue of Jupiter Pen. In the early pilgrimages to Rome this became a place of some importance. Later on, marauding armies of Goths, Saracens, and Hungarians, successively passing through, destroyed this refuge. In the days of Bernard the pass was filled with a horde of brigands, French, Italians, Saracens, and Jews, who had cast aside all religious faith of their fathers, and had re-established the worship of the demon in the temple of Jupiter Pen.

The old manuscripts tell us that in the middle of the tenth century the demons were in full sway on these mountains; that through the mouth of the statue of Jupiter the worst of lies and blasphemies were spoken to those who came to consult it. These worshipers of strange old gods lived by plunder, and exacted toll of all who came through the pass. The same conditions existed on the Graian Alps to the southward. On one of these mountain passes, some fifty miles from Mont Joux, there lived a rich man named Polycarpe. He, too, did homage to Jupiter, and on the summit of a tall column which he built in the pass he had placed a splendid diamond, which he called the " Eye of Jove." People came from great distances to be healed by its magic glance, and the mountain on which he dwelt was the mountain of the Columna Jovis. This became changed, in time, to Colonne Joux, the Mountain of the Column of Jove. And the demons of these two heights, the Mountain of Jove and the Column of Jove, sent down their baleful call of defiance to the valley over which Bernard ruled as Archdeacon of Aosta.

It came to pass that a troop of ten French travelers crossed over the pass of Mont Joux. In the pass they were attacked by marauders, and one of their number was carried away captive. When they came down to Aosta, Bernard, the Archdeacon, fearlessly offered to go back with them to attack the giant of the mountain, to rescue their friend, and to replace the standard of the cross over the altar of the demon.

That night, so says the old chronicle, Saint Nicholas appeared to him in the garb of a pilgrim and said: " Bernard, let us attack these mountains. We shall put the demon to flight. We shall overturn this statue of Jupiter, which the demons have taken possession of to bring trouble among Christians. We will destroy it, and we will destroy the column and its diamond, and in their place we will build two refuges for the use of the pilgrims who cross the two mountains. Go thou, as the tenth one in this band; then wilt thou conjure the demons. Thou shalt bind the statue with a blessed stole, and its ruins will mingle with the chaos of the mountains. Thus shalt thou destroy the power of evil to the day of judgment."

And in proof of the thoroughness with which Bernard performed his work, it is told that a spiritualist who took pleasure in tipping tables came through the pass in 1857. The monks were incredulous of his powers, and he wished to convince them by an actual experience. His efforts were all in vain. The tables, the record tells us, were quiet as the rocks. The traveler, astonished, said: " This is the **first** time they have failed to obey me." And thus, says the record, the pledge of Saint Nicholas was accomplished. The enemy had never more an entrance into the mountain.

When Bernard and his followers reached Mont Joux, they found the mountain filled with fog and storm, but his heart was undaunted. Passing boldly between the guards of the temple, he flung, so the story says, his blessed stole over the neck of the statue of Jupiter. It changed at once into an iron chain, against which the statue, now become a huge demon-monster, struggled in vain. The good man overturned it and flung it at his feet. With the same chain he bound the high priest who guarded the demon. The struggle was short, but decisive. In a few minutes, so the chronicle says, Bernard had banished the demon of Mont Joux and his accomplices to eternal snow and ice to the end of time, and had commanded them to cease forever their evil doings on the mountain.

An old painting in the Hospice shows this scene in vivid portrait. Bernard stands erect and fearless, his fine face lit up by celestial zeal, his bare head surrounded by a halo, a pilgrim's staff in his right hand, the stole, now become a chain, in his left, while one foot is on the breast of the demon, which gasps helpless at his feet. The demon has the body of a man, covered with a wolf's rough, shaggy hair, his fingers and toes ending in sharp claws, a long tail, rough and scaly, like the tail of a rat, coiled snake-like above his legs, the head and ears of a wolf, the horns of a goat, and on his back an indefinable outgrowth, perhaps the framework of a horrible pair of wings, its long tongue thrust out from between its bloody teeth. He was certainly a gruesome creature.

And thus it came to pass in the year 970, in the place of the temple of Jupiter Pen, but at the other end of the lake, and in the very summit of the pass, was built the Hospice of the Great Saint Bernard. From that day to this, almost a thousand years, the work of doing good to men has been humbly and patiently carried on.

Not long afterward, in a similar way, Bernard attacked the Graian Alps, overthrew the column of Jupiter, crushed its bright diamond to the finest dust, which he scattered in the winds, and built in its place a second Hospice, which, with the pass, has borne ever since the name of the Little Saint Bernard.

Silver and gold, the builders of this Hospice had none. Ever since the beginning, they have exercised their charities at the expense of those who

SAINT BERNARD AND THE DEMON.

cared for the Lord's work. All who pass by are treated alike. Those who are received into the Hospice can leave much or little — something or nothing, whatever they please,— to carry the same same help to others.

In the book of the good Saint Francis de Sales long ago, so the chronicle says, these words were written:

"There are many degrees in charity. To lend to the poor, this is the first degree. To give to the poor is a higher degree. Still higher to give one-self; to devote one's life to the service of the poor. Hospitality, when necessity is not extreme, is a counsel, and to receive the stranger is its first de-gree. But to go out on the roads to find and help, as Abraham did, this is a grade still higher. Still higher is to live in dangerous places, to serve, aid, and save the passers-by; to attend, lodge, succor, and save from danger the travelers, who else would die in cold and storm. This is the work of the noble friend of God, who founded the hospitals on the two mountains, now for this called by his name, Great Saint Bernard, in the diocese of Sion, and the Little Saint Bernard, in the Tarentaise."

And so the Hospice was built, and in the enthu-siastic words of a chronicle of the times, "Tears and sorrow were banished, peace and joy have replaced them; abundance has made there her abode; the terrors have disappeared, and there reigns eternal springtime. Instead of hell, you will find there paradise." Not quite paradise, perhaps, so far as the elements are concerned, but a dozen kindly men, a legion of dogs, big, cheerful, and noisy, a warm fire, a simple meal, and a God-speed to all men, whatever their race, or creed, or temper.

I need add but a word more of the history of Bernard himself. One day an old man and his wife came up to visit the Hospice and to pay their respects to the monk who had founded it. Bernard met them there, and at once recognized his father and mother. He received them sympathetically, and they told him the story of their lost son. Bernard spoke to them tenderly of the work to which God must have called him. He told them they should rejoice that their child had been found worthy of his purposes, and after a time they seemed to become reconciled, and felt that He doeth all things well. Then Bernard told them who he was, and when after many days they went away from the Hospice, they left the money to build in each of them a chapel.

Bernard died in the year 1007, at the age of eighty-three. His last words were these: "O Lord,

I give my soul into thy hands." The words, "The saint is dead," passed on from mouth to mouth throughout these Alpine regions. The peasants had canonized him already a hundred years before the sanctity of his work was officially recognized at Rome.

The story of his burial is again marked by miracles. Rich men vied with each other in making funeral offerings. One gave him a magnificent stone coffin, but this man had been a usurer. Usury was a sin abhorred by Saint Bernard, and the people found that no force or persuasion could place his body within this coffin. So another tomb, less pretentious, but more worthy, was found. At the end Bernard's remains were divided among the churches, each of whom claimed him as its own. To the Hospice fell his ring and his cup, a tooth, and a few finger-bones, and, most important of all, his name — the "Great Saint Bernard."

The chronicles give a long list of miracles which since then have been wrought in his name. These are for the most part wonderful healings, the stilling of storms, the bringing of rain, the driving away of grasshoppers. However, men are prone always to look for the miracle in the things that are of least moment. The life and work of the

man was the real miracle, not the flight of grasshoppers. The miracle of all time is the power of
humanity when it works in harmony with the laws
and purposes of God. Consecrated to God's work,
and by the work's own severity protected through
the centuries from corruption and temptation, the
work of the monk of Aosta has outlasted palaces
and thrones. Through the influence of charity, and
piety, and truth, the demon has been driven from
these mountains. When the love of man joins to
the love of God, all spirits of evil vanish as mist
before the morning sun.

THE LAST OF THE PURITANS.

THE LAST OF THE PURITANS.*

I HAVE a word to say of Thoreau, and of an episode which brought his character into bold relief, and which has fairly earned for him a place in American history, as well as in our literature.

I do not wish now to give any account of the life of Thoreau. In the preface to his volume called "Excursions" you will find a biographical sketch, written by the loving hand of Mr. Emerson, his neighbor and friend. Neither shall I enter into any justification of Thoreau's peculiar mode of life, nor shall I describe the famous cabin in the pine woods by Walden Pond, already becoming the Mecca of the Order of Saunterers, whose great prophet was Thoreau. His profession of land-surveyor was one naturally adopted by him; for to him every hill and forest was a being, each with its own individuality. This profession kept him in the fields and woods, with the sky over his head and the mold under his feet. It paid him the money needed for his daily wants, and he cared for no more.

* Address before the California State Normal School, at San José, 1892.

He seldom went far away from Concord, and, in a half-playful way, he used to view everything in the world from a Concord standpoi   All the grandest trees grew there and all the rarest flowers, and nearly all the phenomena of nature could be observed at Concord.

"Nothing can be hoped of you," he said, "if this bit of mold under your feet is not sweeter to you than any other in this world — in any world."

Although one of the most acute of observers, Thoreau was never reckoned among the scientific men of his time. He was never a member of any Natural History Society, nor of any Academy of Sciences, bodies which, in a general way, he held in not altogether unmerited contempt. When men band together for the study of nature, they first draft a long constitution, with its attendant by-laws, and then proceed to the election of officers, and, by and by, the study of nature becomes subordinate to the maintenance of the organization.

In technical scientific work, Thoreau took little pleasure. It is often pedantic, often bloodless, and often it is a source of inspiration only to him by whom the work is done. Animals and plants were interesting to him, not in their structure and genealogical affinities, but in their relations to his

mind. He loved wild things, not alone for themselves, but for the tonic effect of their savagery upon
him.

"I wish to speak a word for nature," he said,
"for absolute freedom and wildness, as contrasted
with a freedom and culture merely civil, to regard
man as an inhabitant, a part and parcel of nature,
rather than as a member of society. I wish to
make an extreme statement; if so, I may make an
emphatic one, for there are enough champions of
civilization. The minister and the school commit-
tees, and every one of you, will take care of that."

To Thoreau's admirers, he is the prophet of the
fields and woods, the interpreter of nature, and his
every word has to them the deepest significance.
He is the man who

> "Lives all alone, close to the bone,
> And where life is sweetest, constantly eatest."

They resent all criticism of his life or his words.
They are impatient of all analysis of his methods
or of his motives, and a word of praise of him is
the surest passport to their good graces.

But the critics sometimes miss the inner harmony which Thoreau's admirers see, and discern only
queer paradoxes and extravagances of statement
where the others hear the voice of nature's oracle.

With most literary men, the power or disposition of those who know or understand their writings is in some degree a matter of literary culture. It is hardly so in the case of Thoreau.

The most illiterate man I know who had ever heard of Thoreau, Mr. Barney Mullins, of Freedom Centre, Outagamie County, Wisconsin, was a most ardent admirer of Thoreau, while the most eminent critic in America, James Russell Lowell, does him scant justice. To Lowell, the finest thoughts of Thoreau are but strawberries from Emerson's garden, and other critics have followed back these same strawberries through Emerson's to still older gardens, among them to that of Sir Thomas Browne.

But, setting the critics aside, let me tell you about Barney Mullins. Twenty years ago, I lived for a year in the northern part of Wisconsin. The snow is very deep in the winter there, and once I rode into town through the snowbanks on a sled drawn by two oxen and driven by Barney Mullins. Barney was born on the banks of Killarney, and he could scarcely be said to speak the English language. He told me that before he came to Freedom Centre he had lived in a town called Concord, in Massachusetts. I asked him if he had happened to know a man there by the name of Henry Thoreau. He at once grew enthusiastic and he said, among other things: "Mr. Thoreau was a land-surveyor in Concord. I knew him well. He had a way of his own, and he didn't care naught about money; but if there was ever a gentleman alive, he was one."

Barney seemed much saddened when I told him that Mr. Thoreau had been dead a dozen years. On parting, he asked me to come out some time to Freedom Centre, and to spend a night with him. He had n't much of a room to offer me, but there was always a place in his house for a friend of Mr. Thoreau. Such is the feeling of this guild of lovers of Thoreau, and some of you may come to belong to it.

Here is a test for you. Thoreau says: "I long ago lost a hound, a bay horse, and a turtle-dove, and am still on their trail. Many are the travelers I have spoken to regarding them, describing their tracks, and what calls they answered to. I have met one or two who have heard the hound and the tramp of the horse, and even seen the dove disappear behind the cloud, and they seemed as anxious to recover them as if they had lost them themselves."

Now, if any of you, in your dreams, have heard the horse, or seen the sunshine on the dove's wings, you may join in the search. If not, you may close the book, for Thoreau has not written for you.

This Thoreau guild is composed, as he himself says, "of knights of a new, or, rather, an old order, not equestrians or chevaliers, not Ritters, or riders, but walkers, a still more ancient and honorable class, I trust."

"I have met," he says, "but one or two persons who understand the art of walking; who had a genius for sauntering, which word is beautifully derived from idle people who roved about the country in the Middle Ages and asked charity, under pretense of going '*à la Sainte Terre*' — a Sainte-terrer, a Holy Lander. They who never go to the Holy Land in their walks, as they pretend, are indeed mere idlers and vagabonds; but they who go there are saunterers, in the good sense. Every walk is a kind of crusade preached by some Peter the Hermit within us, to go forth and reconquer this Holy Land from the hands of the Infidels.

"It is true that we are but faint-hearted crusaders, who undertake no persevering, never-ending enterprises. Our expeditions are but tours, and come round again at evening to the old hearth-

side from which we set out. Half the walk is but
retracing our steps. We should go forth on the
shortest walk, perchance, in the spirit of undying
adventure, never to return, prepared to send back
our embalmed hearts only as relics to our desolate
kingdoms. If you are ready to leave father and
mother, and brother and sister, and wife and child,
and friends; if you have paid your debts, and made
your will, and settled all your affairs, and are a
free man, you are ready for a walk."

Though a severe critic of conventional follies,
Thoreau was always a hopeful man; and no finer
rebuke to the philosophy of Pessimism was ever
given than in these words of his: "I know of no
more encouraging fact than the unquestionable
ability of a man to elevate his life by a conscious
endeavor. It is something to be able to paint a
particular picture, or to carve a statue, and so make
a few objects beautiful; but it is far more glorious
to carve and paint the very atmosphere and me-
dium through which we look. This, morally, we
can do."

But it is not of Thoreau as a saunterer, or as a
naturalist, or as an essayist, that I wish to speak,
but as a moralist, and this in relation to American
politics. Thoreau lived in a dark day of our politi-

cal history. At one time he made a declaration of independence in a small way, and refused allegiance and poll-tax to a Government built on a corner-stone of human slavery. Because of this he was put into jail, where he remained one night, and where he made some curious observations on his townspeople as viewed from the inside of the bars. Emerson came along in the morning, and asked him what he was there for. " Why are *you* not in here, Mr. Emerson?" was his reply; for it seemed to him that no man had the right to be free in a country where some men were slaves.

"Voting for the right," Thoreau said, "is doing nothing for it; it is only expressing feebly your desire that right should prevail." He would not for an instant recognize that political organization as his government which was the slave's government also. "In fact," he said, "I will quietly, after my fashion, declare war with the State. Under a government which imprisons any unjustly, the true place for a just man is also a prison. I know this well, that if one thousand, if one hundred, or if one *honest man* in this State of Massachusetts, ceasing to remain in this co-partnership, should be locked up in the county jail therefor, it would be the abolition of slavery in America. It matters not how small the beginning may seem to be, what is once well done is done forever."

Thoreau's friends paid his taxes for him, and he was set free, so that the whole affair seemed like a joke. Yet, as Stevenson says, "If his example had been followed by a hundred, or by thirty of his followers, it would have greatly precipitated the era of freedom and justice. We feel the misdeeds of our country with so little fervor, for we are not witnesses to the suffering they cause. But when we see them awake an active horror in our fellow-man; when we see a neighbor prefer to lie in prison than be so much as passively implicated in their perpetration, even the dullest of us will begin to realize them with a quicker pulse."

In the feeling that a wrong, no matter how great, must fall before the determined assault of a man, no matter how weak, Thoreau found the reason for his action. The operation of the laws of God is like an incontrollable torrent. Nothing can stand before them; but the work of a single man may set the torrent in motion which will sweep away the accumulations of centuries of wrong.

There is a long chapter in our national history which is not a glorious record. Most of us are too young to remember much of politics under the

Fugitive Slave Law, or to understand the defer-
ence which politicians of every grade then paid to
the peculiar institution. It was in those days in
the Middle West that Kentucky blackguards, backed
by the laws of the United States, and aided not by
Northern blackguards alone, but by many of the
best citizens of those States, chased runaway slaves
through the streets of our Northern capitals.

And not the politicians alone, but the teachers
and preachers, took their turn in paying tribute to
Cæsar. We were told that the Bible itself was a
champion of slavery. Two of our greatest theologians in the North declared, in the name of the
Higher Law, that slavery was a holy thing, which
the Lord, who cursed Canaan, would ever uphold.

In those days there came a man from the West—
a tall, gaunt, grizzly, shaggy-haired, God-fearing
man, a son of the Puritans, whose ancestors came
over on the Mayflower. A dangerous fanatic or
lunatic, he was called, and, with the aid of a few
poor negroes whom he had stolen from slavery, he
defied the power of this whole slave-catching United
States. A little square brick building, once a sort
of car-shop, stands near the railway station in the
town of Harper's Ferry, with the mountain wall
not far behind it, and the Potomac River running

JOHN BROWN.

below. And from this building was fired the shot which pierced the heart of slavery. And the Governor of Virginia captured this man, and took him out and hung him, and laid his body in the grave, where it still lies moldering. But there was part of him not in the jurisdiction of Virginia, a part which they could neither hang nor bury; and, to the infinite surprise of the Governor of Virginia, his soul went marching on.

When they heard in Concord that John Brown had been captured, and was soon to be hung, Thoreau sent notice through the city that he would speak in the public hall on the condition and character of John Brown, on Sunday evening, and invited all to be present.

The Republican Committee and the Committee of the Abolitionists sent word to him that this was no time to speak; to discuss such matters then was premature and inadvisable. He replied: "I did not send to you for advice, but to tell you that I am going to speak." The selectmen of Concord dared neither grant nor refuse him the hall. At last they ventured to lose the key in a place where they thought he could find it.

This address of Thoreau, "A Plea for Captain John Brown," should be a classic in American history. We do not always realize that the time of American history is now. The dates of the settlement of Jamestown, and Plymouth, and St. Augustine do not constitute our history. Columbus did not discover us. In a high sense, the true America is barely thirty years old, and its first President was Abraham Lincoln.

We in the North are a little impatient at times, and our politicians, who are not always our best citizens, mutter terrible oaths, especially in the month of October, because the South is not yet wholly regenerate, because not all which sprang from the ashes of the slave-pen were angels of light.

But let us be patient while the world moves on. Forty years ago not only the banks of the Yazoo and the Chattahoochee, but those of the Hudson, and the Charles, and the Wabash, were under the lash. On the eve of John Brown's hanging not half a dozen men in the city of Concord, the most intellectual town in New England, the home of Emerson, and Hawthorne, and Alcott, dared say that they felt any respect for the man or sympathy for the cause for which he died.

I wish to quote a few passages from this "Plea for Captain John Brown." To fully realize its power, you should read it all for yourselves. You must put yourselves back into history, now already seeming almost ancient history to us, to the period when Buchanan was President—the terrible sultry lull just before the great storm. You must picture the audience of the best people in Massachusetts, half-sympathizing with Captain Brown, half-afraid of being guilty of treason in so doing. You must picture the speaker, with his clear-cut, earnest features and penetrating voice. No preacher, no politician, no professional reformer, no Republican, no Democrat; a man who never voted; a naturalist whose companions were the flowers and the birds, the trees and the squirrels. It was the voice of Nature in protest against slavery and in plea for Captain Brown.

"My respect for my fellow-men," said Thoreau, "is not being increased these days. I have noticed the cold-blooded way in which men speak of this event, as if an ordinary malefactor, though one of unusual pluck, 'the gamest man I ever saw,' the Governor of Virginia said, had been caught and was about to be hung. He was not thinking of his foes when the Governor of Virginia thought he looked so brave.

"It turns what sweetness I have to gall to hear the remarks of some of my neighbors. When we heard at first that he was dead, one of my townsmen observed that 'he dieth as the fool dieth,' which, for an instant, suggested a likeness in him dying to my neighbor living. Others, craven-hearted, said, disparagingly, that he threw his life away because he resisted the Government. Which way have they thrown their lives, pray?

"I hear another ask, Yankee-like, 'What will he gain by it?' as if he expected to fill his pockets by the enterprise. If it does not lead to a surprise party, if he does not get a new pair of boots or a vote of thanks, it must be a failure. But he won't get anything. Well, no; I don't suppose he could get four-and-sixpence a day for being hung, take the year around, but he stands a chance to save his soul — and such a soul! — which you do not. You can get more in your market for a quart of milk than a quart of blood, but yours is not the market heroes carry their blood to.

"Such do not know that like the seed is the fruit, and that in the moral world, when good seed is planted, good fruit is inevitable; that when you plant or bury a hero in his field, a crop of heroes is sure to spring up. This is a seed of such force and vitality, it does not ask our leave to germinate.

"A man does a brave and humane deed, and on all sides we hear people and parties declaring, 'I did n't do it, nor countenance him to do it in any conceivable way. It can't fairly be inferred from my past career.' Ye need n't take so much pains, my friends, to wash your skirts of him. No one will ever be convinced that he was any creature of yours. He went and came, as he himself informs us, under the anspices of John Brown, and nobody else.

"'All is quiet in Harper's Ferry,' say the journals. What is the character of that calm which follows when the law and the slaveholder prevail? I regard this event as a touchstone designed to bring out with glaring distinctness the character of this Government. We needed to be thus assisted to see it by the light of history. It needed to see itself. When a government puts forth its strength on the side of injustice, as ours, to maintain slavery and kill the liberators of the slave, it reveals itself simply as brute force. It is more manifest than ever that tyranny rules. I see this Government to be effectually allied with France and Austria in oppressing mankind.

"The only government that I recognize—and it matters not how few are at the head of it, or how small its army,—is the power that establishes justice in the land, never that which establishes injustice. What shall we think of a government to which all the truly brave and just men in the land are enemies, standing between it and those whom it oppresses?

"Treason! Where does such treason take its rise? I cannot help thinking of you as ye deserve, ye governments! Can you dry up the fountain of thought? High treason, when it is resistance to tyranny here below, has its origin in the power that makes and forever re-creates man. When you have caught and hung all its human rebels, you have accomplished nothing but your own guilt. You have not struck at the fountain-head. The same indignation which cleared the temple once will clear it again.

"I hear many condemn these men because they were so few. When were the good and the brave ever in the majority? Would you have had him wait till that time came? Till you and I came over to him? The very fact that he had no rabble or troop of hirelings about him, would alone distinguish him from ordinary heroes. His company was small, indeed, because few could be found worthy to pass muster. Each one who there laid down his life for the poor and oppressed was a picked man, called out of many thousands, if not millions. A man of principle, of rare courage and devoted humanity, ready to sacrifice his life at any moment for the benefit of his fellow-man; it may be doubted if there were as many more their equals in the country; for their leader, no doubt, had scoured the land far and wide, seeking to swell his troop. These alone were ready to step between the oppressor and the oppressed. Surely they were the very best men you could select to be hung! That was the greatest compliment their country could pay them. They were ripe for her gallows. She has tried a long time; she has hung a good many, but never found the right one before.

"When I think of him and his six sons and his son-in-law enlisted for this fight, proceeding coolly, reverently, humanely to work, for months, if not years, summering and wintering the thought, without expecting any reward but a good conscience, while almost all America stood ranked on the other side, I say again that it affects me as a sublime spectacle.

" If he had had any journal advocating his cause, any organ monotonously and wearisomely playing the same old tune and then passing around the hat, it would have been fatal to his efficiency. If he had acted in such a way as to be let alone by the Government, he might have been suspected. It was the fact that the tyrant must give place to him, or he to the tyrant, that distinguished him from all the reformers of the day that I know.

"This event advertises me that there is such a fact as death, the possibility of a man's dying. It seems as if no man had ever died in America before. If this man's acts and words do not create a revival, it will be the severest possible satire on words and acts that do.

"It is the best news that America has ever heard. It has already quickened the feeble pulse of the North, and infused more generous blood in her veins than any number of years of what is called political and commercial prosperity. How many a man who was lately contemplating suicide has now something to live for!

" I am here to plead his cause with you. I plead not for his life, but for his character, his immortal life, and so it becomes your cause wholly, and it is not his in the least.

"Some eighteen hundred years ago Christ was crucified; this morning, perchance, Captain Brown was hung. These are the two ends of the chain which is not without its links. He is not Old Brown any longer; he is an angel of light. I see now that it was necessary that the bravest and humanest man in all the country should be hung. Perhaps he saw it himself. I almost fear that I may yet hear of his deliverance, doubting if a prolonged life, if any life, can do as much good as his death.

"'Misguided! Garrulous! Insane! Vindictive!' So you write in your easy chairs, and thus he, wounded, responds from the floor of the Armory— clear as a cloudless sky, true as the voice of Nature is! 'No man sent me here. It was my own promptings and that of my Maker. I acknowledge no master in human form.'

"And in what a sweet and noble strain he proceeds, addressing his captors, who stand over him.

"' I think, my friends, you are guilty of a great wrong against God and humanity, and it would be perfectly right for any one to interfere with you so far as to free those you willfully and wickedly hold in bondage. I have yet to learn that God is any respecter of persons.

" ' I pity the poor in bondage, who have none to help them; that is why I am here, not to gratify personal animosity, revenge, or vindictive spirit. It is my sympathy with the oppressed and the wronged that are as good as you are, and as precious in the sight of God.

" ' I wish to say, furthermore, that you had better, all of you people at the South, prepare yourselves for a settlement of that question, that must come up for settlement sooner than you are prepared for it. The sooner you are prepared the better. You may dispose of me now very easily — I am nearly disposed of already, — but this question is still to be settled, this negro question, I mean; the end of that is not yet.' "

"I foresee the time," said Thoreau, " when the painter will paint that scene, no longer going to Rome for his subject. The poet will sing it; the historian record it; and, with the Landing of the Pilgrims and the Declaration of Independence, it will be the ornament of some future national gallery, when at least the present form of slavery shall be no more here. We shall then be at liberty to weep for Captain Brown. Then, and not till then, we will take our revenge."

A few years ago, while on a tramp through the North Woods, I came out through the forests of North Elba, to the old "John Brown Farm." Here John Brown lived for many years, and here he tried to establish a colony of freed slaves in the pure air of the mountains. Here, too, his family remained through the stirring times when he took part in the bloody struggles that made and kept Kansas free.

The little old brown farmhouse stands on the edge of the great woods, a few miles to the north of the highest peaks of the Adirondacks. There is nothing unusual about the house. You will find a dozen such in a few hours' walk almost anywhere in the mountain parts of New England or New York. It stands on a little hill, "in a sightly place," as they say in that region, with no shelter of trees around it.

At the foot of the hill in a broad curve flows the River Au Sable, small and clear and cold, and full of trout. It is not far above that the stream takes its rise in the dark Indian Pass, the only place in these mountains where the ice of winter lasts all summer long. The same ice on the one side sends forth the Au Sable, and on the other feeds the fountain head of the infant Hudson River.

In the little dooryard in front of the farmhouse is the historic spot where John Brown's body still lies moldering. There is not even a grave of his own. His bones lie with those of his father, and the short record of his life and death is crowded on

THE JOHN BROWN HOMESTEAD, NORTH ELBA, N. Y.

the foot of his father's tombstone. Near by, in the little yard, lies a huge, wandering boulder, torn off years ago by the glaciers from the granite hills that hem in Indian Pass. The boulder is ten feet or more in diameter, large enough to make the farmhouse behind it seem small in comparison. On its upper surface, in letters two feet long, which can be read plainly for a mile away, is cut the simple name—

JOHN BROWN.

This is John Brown's grave, and the place, the boulder, and the inscription are alike fitting to the man he was.

Dust to dust; ashes to ashes; granite to granite; the last of the Puritans!

JOHN BROWN'S GRAVE.

A KNIGHT OF THE ORDER OF POETS.*

"In London I saw two pictures. One was of a woman. You would not mistake it for any of the Greek goddesses. It had a splendor and majesty such as Phidias might have given to a woman Jupiter. But not terrible. The culmination of the awful beauty was in an expression of matchless compassion. If there had been other figures, they must have been suffering humanity at her feet.

"The other was also of a woman. Whose face it is hard to say. Not the Furies, not Lady Macbeth, not Catherine de Medici, not Philip the Second, not Nero, not any face you have ever seen, but a gathering up from all the faces you have seen — the greatness, the splendor, the savagery, the greed, the pride, the hate, the mercilessness, into one colossal, terrifyingly Satanic woman-face. The first was clothed in a simple, soft, white robe; the other in a befitting tragic splendor, mostly blood-red. I looked from one to the other. What immeasurable distance between them! What single point have they in common? But as I look back and forth I seem to see a certain formal similarity. It grows upon me. I am incredulous. I am appalled. Then one touches me and whispers: 'They are the same. It is the Church.' In London I saw this — in the air."— WILLIAM LOWE BRYAN.

FOUR centuries ago began the great struggle for freedom of thought which has made our modern civilization possible. I wish here to give something of the story of a man who in his day was not the least in this conflict—a man who

---

*For many of the details of the life of Hutten, and for most of the quotations from Hutten's writings given in this paper, the writer is indebted to the excellent memoir by David Friedrich Strauss, entitled "Ulrich von Hutten." (Fourth Edition: Bonn, 1878.) No attempt has been made to give here an account of Hutten's writings, only a few of the more noteworthy being mentioned.

dared to think and act for himself when thought and act were costly — Ulrich von Hutten.

Near Frankfort-on-the-Main, on a sharp pinnacle of rock above the little railway station of Vollmerz, may still be found the scanty ruins of an old castle which played a brave part in German history before it was destroyed in the Thirty Years War.

In this castle of Steckelberg, in the year 1488, was born Ulrich von Hutten. He was the last of a long line of Huttens of Steckelberg, strong men who knew not fear, who had fought for the Emperor in all lands whither the imperial eagle had flown, and who, when the empire was at peace, had fought right merrily with their neighbors on all sides. Robber-knights they were, no doubt, some or all of them; but in those days all was fair in love and in war. And this line of warriors centered in Ulrich von Hutten, and with him it ended. "The wild kindred has gone out with this its greatest."

Ulrich was the eldest son, and bore his father's name. But he was not the son his father had dreamed of. Slender of figure, short of stature, and weak of limb, Ulrich seemed unworthy of his burly ancestry. The horse, the sword, and the lute were not for him. He tried hard to master them and to succeed in all things worthy of a knight. But he was strong only with his books. At last to his books his father consigned him, and, sorely disappointed, he sent Ulrich to the monastery of Fulda to be made a priest.

A wise man, Eitelwolf von Stein, became his friend, and pointed out to him a life braver than that of a priest, more noble than that of a knight, the life of a scholar. To Hutten's father Eitelwolf wrote: "Would you bury a genius like that in the cloister? He must be a man of letters." But the father had decided once for all. Ulrich must never return to Steckelberg unless he came back as a priest. And the son took his fate in his own hands, and fled from Fulda, to make his way as a scholar in a world in which scholarship received scanty recognition.

At the same time another young man whose history was to be interwoven with his own, Martin Luther, fled from the wickedness and deceit of this same world to the solitude of the monastery of Erfurth. By very different paths they came at last to work in the same cause, and their modes of action were not less different.

To the University of Cologne Hutten went, and with the students of that day he was trained in the mysteries of scholasticism, and in the Latin of the schoolmen and the priests. Wonderful problems they pondered over, and they used to write long arguments in Latin for or against propositions which came nowhere within the domain of fact. That scholarship stood related to reality, and that it must find its end and justification in action was no part of the philosophy of those times.

But Hutten and his friends cared little for scholastic puzzles and they gave themselves to the study of the beauties of Latin poetry and to the newly opened mine of the literature of Greece. They delighted in Virgil and Lucian, and still more in Homer and Æschylus.

The Turks had conquered Constantinople, and the fall of the Greek Empire had driven many learned Greeks to the West of Europe. There some of the scholars received them with open arms, and eagerly learned from them to read Homer and Aristotle in the original tongue, and the New Testament also. Those who followed these studies came to be known as Humanists. But most of the universities and the monasteries in Germany looked upon this revival of Greek culture as pernicious and antichristian. Poetry they despised. The Latin Vulgate met their religious needs, and Greek was only another name for Paganism. The party name of Obscurantists ("*Dunkelmänner*") was given to these, and this name has remained with them on the records of history.

In the letters of one of Hutten's comrades we find this confession of faith, which is interesting as expressing the feelings of young men of that time: "There is but one God, but he has many forms, and many names—Jupiter, Sol, Apollo, Moses, Christ, Luna, Ceres, Proserpine, Tellus, Mary. But be careful how you say that. One must disclose these things in secret, like Eleusinian mysteries. In matters of religion, you must use the cover of fables and riddles. You, with Jupiter's grace (that is, the grace of the best and greatest god), can despise the lesser gods in silence. When I say Jupiter, I mean Christ and the true God. The coat and the beard and the bones of Christ I worship not. I worship the living God, who wears no coat nor beard, and left no bones upon the earth."

Hutten wished to know the world, not from books only, but to see all cities and lands; to measure himself with other men; to rise above those less worthy. The danger of such a course seemed to him only the greater attraction. Content to him was laziness; love of home but a dog's delight in a warm fire. " I live," he said, " in no place rather than another; my home is everywhere."

So he tramped through Germany to the northward, and had but a sorry time. In his own mind he was a scholar, a poet, a knight of the noblest blood of Germany; to others he was a little sickly and forlorn vagrant. Never strong of body, he was stricken by a miserable disease which filled his life with a succession of attacks of fever. He was shipwrecked on the Baltic Sea, sick and forlorn in Pomerania, and at last he was received in charity in the house of Henning Lötz, professor of law at Greifeswald.

This action has given Lötz's name immortality, for it is associated with the first of those fiery poems of Hutten which, in their way, are unique in literature. For Hutten was restless and proud, and was not to be content with bread and butter and a new suit of clothes. This independence was displeasing to the professor, who finally, in utter disgust, turned Hutten out of doors in midwinter. When the boy had tramped a while in storm and slush, two servants of Lötz overtook him on the road and robbed him of his money and clothing. In a wretched plight he reached a little inn in Rostock, in Mecklenberg. Here the professors in

the university received him kindly, and made provision for his needs. Then he let loose the fury
of his youthful anger on Lötz. As ever, his poetic
genius rose with his wrath, and the more angry
he became the greater was he as a poet.

Two volumes he published, ringing the changes
of his contempt and hatred of Lötz, at the same
time praising the virtues of those who had found
in him a kindred spirit. A "knight of the order
of poets," he styles himself, and to all Humanists,
to the "fellow-feeling among free spirits" ("*Gem-
eingeist unter freien Geistern*") he appeals for sympathy in his struggle with Lötz.

He had, indeed, not found a foeman worthy of
his steel, but he had shown what a finely tempered
blade he bore. Foemen enough he found in later
times, and his steel had need of all its sharpness
and temper. And it never failed him to the last.

Meanwhile he wandered to Vienna, giving lectures there on the art of poetry. But poetry was
abhorred by the schoolmen everywhere, and the
students of the university were forbidden to attend
his lectures. He then went to Italy. When he
reached Pavia, he found the city in the midst of a
siege, surrounded by a hostile French army. He
fell ill of a fever, and giving himself up for dead,

he composed the famous epitaph for himself, of which I give a rough translation:

Here, also be it said, a life of ill-fortune is ended;
  By evil pursued on the water; beset by wrong upon land.
Here lie Hutten's bones; he, who had done nothing wrongful,
  Was wickedly robbed of his life by the sword in a French-
    man's hand.
By Fate, decided that he should see unlucky days only;
  Decided that even these days could never be many or long;
Hemmed in by danger and death, he forsook not serving the
    muses,
  And as well as he could, he rendered this service in song.

The Frenchman's sword did not rob him of his life. The Frenchman's hand took only his money, which was not much, and again sent him adrift. He now set his pen to writing epigrams on the Emperor, wherein Maximilian was compared to the eagle which should devour the frogs in the swamps of Venice. Meanwhile he enlisted as a common soldier in Maximilian's army.

In Italy, the abuses of the Papacy attracted his attention. Officials of the Church were then engaged in extending the demand for indulgences. The sale of pardons "straight from Rome, all hot," was becoming a scandal in Christendom. All this roused the wrath of Hutten, who attacked the Pope himself in his songs:

" Heaven now stands for a price to be peddled and sold,
But what new folly is this, as though the fiat of Heaven
Needed an earthly witness, an earthly warrant and seal!"

More prosperous times followed, and we find Hutten honored as a poet, living in the court of the Archbishop of Mainz. At this time a cousin, Hans Hutten, a young man of great courage and promise, was a knight in the service of Ulrich, Duke of Würtemberg. He was a favorite of the Duke, and he and his young wife were the life of the Würtemburg court. And Duke Ulrich once came to Hans and threw himself at his feet, begging that this wife, whom he loved, should be given over wholly to him. Hans Hutten answered the Duke like a man, and the Duke arose with murder in his heart. Afterward, when they were hunting in a wood, he stabbed Hans Hutten in the back with his sword.

All this came to the ear of Ulrich Hutten in Mainz. Love for his cousin, love for his name and family, love for freedom and truth, all urged him to avenge the murdered Hans. The wrongs the boy had suffered from the coarse-hearted Professor Lötz became as nothing beside this great crime against the Huttens and against manhood.

In all the history of invective, I know of nothing so fierce as Hutten's appeal against Duke Ulrich.

In five different pamphlets his crime was described to the German people, and all good men, from the Emperor down, were called on to help him in his struggle against the Duke of Würtemberg.

"I envy you your fame, you murderer," he wrote. "A year will be named for you, and there shall be a day set off for you. Future generations shall read, for those who are born this year, that they were born in the year stained by the ineffaceable shame of Germany. You will come into the calendar, scoundrel. You will enrich history. Your deed is immortal, and you will be remembered in all future time. You have had your ambition, and you shall never be forgotten."

This struggle lasted long. Finally, after many appeals, the German nobles rose in arms and besieged Stuttgart, and Duke Ulrich was driven from the land he had disgraced.

Again Hutten visited Italy, this time by a partial reconciliation with his father, who would overlook his failure to become a priest if he would study law at Rome. At about this time Luther visited Rome. He came, at first, in a spirit of reverence; but, at last, he wrote: "*Wenn es gibt eine Hölle, Roma ist darauf gebaut.*" ("If there is a hell, Rome is built on it.")

ULRICH VON HUTTEN.

The impression on Hutten was scarcely less vivid. Little by little he began to see in the Pope of Rome a criminal greater that Professor Lötz, greater than Duke Ulrich, one who could devour not one cousin only, but the whole German people and nation. "For three hundred years," said he, "the Pope and the schoolmen have been covering the teachings of Christ with a mass of superstitious ceremonies and wicked books." These feelings were poured out in an appeal to the German rulers to shake off the yoke, and no longer send their money to "Simon of Rome."

Hutten's friends tried to quiet him. He was a man not of free thought only, but of free speech, and knew no concealment. Milder men in those times, as later Melancthon and Erasmus, were full of admiration of Hutten, and valued his skill and force. But they were afraid of him, and fearful always that the best of causes should be wrecked in his hands.

At this time, at the age of twenty-five, Hutten is described as a small, thin man, of homely features, with blonde hair and black beard. His pale face wore a severe, almost wild, expression. His speech was sharp, often terrible. Yet with those whom he loved and respected his voice had a frank and win-ning charm. He had but few friends, but they were fast ones. His personal character, so far as records go, was singularly pure, and not often in his writings does he strike a coarse or unclean note.

In these days, the two most learned men in Germany were Erasmus and Reuchlin. They were leaders of the Humanists, skilled in Greek, and even in the Hebrew tongue, and were called by Hutten " the two eyes of Germany." A Jew named Pfefferkorn, who had become converted to Christianity, was filled with an unholy zeal against his fellow-Jews who had not been converted. Among other things, he asked an edict from the Emperor that all Jewish books in Germany should be destroyed. Reuchlin was a Hebrew scholar. He had written a Hebrew grammar, and was learned in the Old Testament, as well as in the Talmud, and other deposits of the ancient lore of the rabbis. The Emperor referred Pfefferkorn's request to Reuchlin for his opinion. Reuchlin decided that there was no valid reason for the destruction of any of the ancient Jewish writings, and only of such modern ones as might be decided by competent scholars to be hostile to Christianity.

This enraged Pfefferkorn and his Obscurantist associates. Pamphlets were written denouncing

Reuchlin, and these were duly answered. A general war of words between the Humanists and Obscurantists began, which, in time, came before the Pope and the Emperor. Reuchlin was regarded in those days as a man of unusual calmness and dignity. Next to Erasmus, he was the most learned scholar in Europe. He would never condescend in his controversies to the coarse terms used by his adversaries. We may learn something of the temper of the times by observing that, in a single pamphlet, as quoted by Strauss, the epithets that the dignified Reuchlin applies to Pfefferkorn are: "A poisonous beast," "a scarecrow," "a horror," "a mad dog," "a horse," "a mule," "a hog," "a fox," "a raging wolf," "a Syrian lion," "a Cerberus," "a fury of hell." In this matter Reuchlin was finally triumphant. This triumph was loudly celebrated by his friend Hutten in another poem, in which the Obscurantists were mercilessly attacked.

We have seen with Hutten's growth a gradual increase in the importance of those to whom he declared himself an enemy. He began as a boy with the obscure Professor Lötz. He ended with the Pope of Rome.

At this time Reuchlin published a volume called *"Epistolæ Clarorum Virorum"* ("letters of illus-

trious men "). It was made up of letters written
by the various learned men of Europe to Reuchlin,
in sympathy with him in his struggle. The title
of this work gave the keynote to a series of letters
called "*Epistolæ Obscurorum Virorum*" ("letters of
obscure men ")—that is, of Obscurantists.

These letters, written by different persons, but
largely by Hutten, are the most remarkable of all
satires of that time.

They are a series of imaginary epistles, supposed
to be addressed by various Obscurantists to a poet
named Ortuinus. They are written with consum-
mate skill, in the degenerate Latin used by the
priests in those days, and they are made to exhibit
all the secret meanness, ignorance, and perversity
of their supposed writers.

The first of these epistles of the "obscure men"
were eagerly read by their supposed associates, the
Obscurantists. Here were men who felt as they felt,
and who were not afraid to speak. The mendicant
friars in England had a day of rejoicing, and a
Dominican friar in Flanders bought all the copies
of the letters he could find to present to his bishop.

But in time even the dullest began to feel the
severity of the satire. The last of these letters
formed the most telling blows ever dealt at the

schoolmen by the men of learning. In one of the
earlier letters we find this question, which may serve
as a type of many others:

A man ate an egg in which a chicken was just
beginning to form, ignorant of that fact, and forgetting that it was Friday. A friend consoles him by
saying that a chicken in that stage counts for no
more than worms in cheese or in cherries, and
these can be eaten even in fasting-time. But the
writer is not satisfied. Worms, he had been told
by a physician, who was also a great naturalist, are
reckoned as fishes, which one can eat on fast-days.
But with all this, he fears that a young chicken
may be really forbidden food, and he asks the help
of the poet Ortuinus to a righteous decision.

Another person writes to Ortuinus: "There is a
new book much talked of here, and, as you are a
poet, you can do us a good service by telling us of
it. A notary told me that this book is the well-
spring of poetry, and that its author, one Homer,
is the father of all poets. And he said there is
another Homer in Greek. I said, 'What is the use
of the Greek? the Latin is much better.' And I
asked, 'What is contained in the book?' And he
said it treats of certain people who are called
Greeks, who carried on a war with some others

called Trojans. And these Trojans had a great
city, and those Greeks besieged it and stayed there
ten years. And the Trojans came out and fought
them till the whole plain was covered with blood
and quite red. And they heard the noise in
heaven, and one of them threw a stone which
twelve men could not lift, and a horse began to
talk and utter prophecies. But I can't believe
that, because it seems impossible, and the book
seems to me not to be authentic. I pray you give
me your opinion."

Another relates the story of his visit to Reuchlin:
"When I came into his house, Reuchlin said,
'Welcome, bachelor; seat yourself.' And he had
a pair of spectacles ('*unum Brillum*') on his nose,
and a book before him curiously written, and I
saw at once that it was neither in German nor
Bohemian, nor yet in Latin. And I said to him,
'Respected Doctor, what do they call that book?'
He answered, 'It is called the Greek Plutarch,
and it treats of philosophy.' And I said, 'Read
some of it, for it must contain wonderful things.'
Then I saw a little book, newly printed, lying on
the floor, and I said to him, 'Respected Doctor,
what lies there?' He answered, 'It is a contro-
versial book, which a friend in Cologne sent me

lately. It is written against me. The theologians in Cologne have printed it, and they say that Johann Pfefferkorn wrote it.' And I said, 'What will you do about it? Will you not vindicate yourself?' And he answered, 'Certainly not. I have been vindicated long ago, and can spend no time on these follies. My eyes are too weak for me to waste their strength on matters which are not useful.'"

We next find Hutten high in the favor of the Emperor Maximilian, by whose order he was crowned poet-laureate of Germany. The wreath of laurel was woven by the fair hands of Constance Peutinger, who was called the handsomest girl in Germany, and with great ceremony she put this wreath on his head in the presence of the Emperor, at Mainz.

Now, for the first time, Hutten seems to have thought seriously of marriage. He writes to a friend, Friedrich Fischer: "I am overcome with a longing for rest, that I may give myself to art. For this, I need a wife who shall take care of me. You know my ways. I cannot be alone, not even by night. In vain they talk to me of the pleasures of celibacy. To me it is loneliness and monotony. I was not born for that. I must have a being who can lead me from sorrows—yes, even from my graver studies; one with whom I can joke and play, and carry on light and happy conversations, that the sharpness of sorrow may be blunted and the heat of anger made mild. Give me a wife, dear Friedrich, and you know what kind of one I want. She must be young, pretty, well educated, serene, tender, patient. Money enough give her, but not too much. For riches I do not seek; and as for blood and birth, she is already noble to whom Hutten gives his hand."

A young woman—Cunigunde Glauburg—was found, and she seemed to meet all requirements. But the mother of the bride was not pleased with the arrangement. Hutten was a "dangerous man," she said, "a revolutionist." "I hope," said Hutten, "that when she comes to know me, and finds in me nothing restless, nothing mutinous, my studies full of humor and wit, that she will look more kindly on me." To a brother of Cunigunde he writes: "Hutten has not conquered many cities, like some of these iron-eaters, but through many lands has wandered with the fame of his name. He has not slain his thousands, like those, but may be none the less loved for that. He does not stalk about on yard-long shin-bones, nor does his gigantic figure frighten travelers; but in strength of spirit he yields to none. He does not glow with the splendor of beauty, but he dares flatter himself that his soul is worthy of love. He does not talk big nor swell himself with boasting, but simply, openly, honestly acts and speaks."

But all his wooing came to naught; another man wedded the fair Cunigunde, and the coming storm of Romish wrath left Hutten no opportunity to turn his attention elsewhere.

The old Pope was now dead, and one of the famous family of Medici, in Florence, had succeeded him as Leo the Tenth. Leo was kindly disposed toward the Humanist studies, and Hutten, as poet of the Humanists, addressed to him directly a remarkable appeal, which made the turning-point in his life, for it placed him openly among those who resisted the Pope.

Recounting to the new Pope Leo all the usurpations which in his judgment had been made, one by one, by his predecessors—all the robberies, impositions, and abuses of the Papacy, from the time of Constantine down—he appeals to Leo, as a wise man and a scholar, to restore stolen power and property, to correct all abuses, to abandon all

temporal power, and become once more the simple
Bishop of Rome. "For there can never be peace
between the robber and the robbed till the stolen
goods are returned."

Now, for the first time, the work of Luther came
to Hutten's attention. The disturbances at Wit-
tenberg were in the beginning treated by all as a
mere squabble of the monks. To Leo the Tenth
this discussion had no further interest than this:
"Brother Martin," being a scholar, was most prob-
ably right. To Hutten, who cared nothing for
doctrinal points, it had no significance; the more
monkish strifes the better—"the sooner would the
enemies eat each other up."

But now Hutten came to recognize in Luther the
apostle of freedom of thought, and in that struggle
of the Reformation he found a nobler cause than
that of the Humanists—in Luther a greater than
Reuchlin. And Hutten never did things by
halves. He entered into the warfare heart and
soul. In 1520 he published his "Roman Trinity,"
his gage of battle against Rome.

He now, like Luther, began to draw his inspiration, as well as his language, not from the classics,
but from the New Testament. A new motto he
took for himself, one which was henceforth ever

on his lips, and which appears again and again in his later writings: "*Jacta est alea*" ("the die is cast"); or, in the stronger German, in which he more often gave it, "*Ich hab's gewagt*" ("I have dared it").

> "Auf dasz ichs nit anheb umsunst
> Wolauf, wir haben Gottes Gunst;
> Wer wollt in solchem bleiben dheim?
> Ich hab's gewagt! das ist mein Reim!"

> "Der niemand grössern Schaden bringt,
> Dann mir als noch die Sach gelingt
> Dahin mich Gott und Wahrheit bringt,
> Ich hab's gewagt."

"So breche ich hindurch, durch breche ich, oder ich falle,
Kämpfend, nach dem ich einmal geworfen das Loos!"

(So break I through the ranks else I die fighting—
Fighting, since once and forever the die I have cast!)

In this motto we have the keynote to his fiery and earnest nature. Convinced that a cause was right, he knew no bounds of caution or policy; he feared no prison or death. "I have dared it!"

"To all free men of Germany," he speaks. "Their tyranny will not last forever; unless all signs deceive me, their power is soon to fail—for already is the axe laid at the root of the tree, and that tree which bears not good fruit will be rooted out, and the vineyard of the Lord will be purified.

That you shall not only hope, but soon see with
your eyes.   Meanwhile, be of good cheer, you men
of Germany.   Not weak, not untried, are your
leaders in the struggle for freedom.   Be not afraid,
neither weaken in the midst of the battle, for
broken at last is the strength of the enemy, for the
cause is righteous, and the rage of tyranny is
already at its height.   Courage, and farewell!
Long live freedom!   I have dared it!"   (*"Lebe die
Freiheit; ich hab's gewagt."*)

Warnings and threats innumerable came to
Hutten, from enemies who feared and hated, from
friends who were fearful and trembling; but he
never flinched.   He had "dared it."   The bull of
excommunication which came from the Pope
frightened him no more than it did Luther.   But
at last he was compelled to retire from the cities,
and he took up his abode in the Castle of Ebernburg, with Franz von Sickingen.

Franz von Sickingen was one of the great nobles
of Germany, and he ruled over a region in the
bend of the Rhine between Worms and Bingen.
His was one of the bravest characters of that
time.   A knight of the highest order, he became
a disciple of Hutten and Luther, and on his help
was the greatest reliance placed by the friends of

the growing reform. His strong Castle of Ebernburg, on the hills above Bingen, was the refuge
of all who were persecuted by the authorities.
The "Inn of Righteousness" ("*Herberge von Ge-
rechtigkeit*"), the Ebernburg was called by Hutten.

The Humanists who had stood with Hutten in
the struggle between Reuchlin and Pfefferkorn saw
with growing concern the gradual transfer of the
field of battle from questions of literature to questions of religion. Reuchlin, growing old and weak,
wrote a letter, disavowing any sympathy with the
new uprisings against the time-honored authority
of the Church. This letter came into Hutten's
hands, and, with all his reverence for his old friend
and master, he could not keep silence.

"Eternal Gods!" he writes. "What do I see?
Have you sunk so deep in weakness and fear, O
Reuchlin! that you cannot endure blame even for
those who have fought for you in time of danger?
Through such shameful subservience do you hope
to reconcile those to whom, if you were a man, you
would never give a friendly greeting, so badly
have they treated you? Yet reconcile them; and if
there is no other way, go to Rome and kiss the feet
of Leo, and then write against us. Yet you shall
see that, against your will, and against the will of

all the godless courtesans, we shall shake off the shameful yoke, and free ourselves from slavery. I am ashamed that I have written so much for you —have done so much for you,—since when it comes to action you have made such a miserable exit from the ranks. From me shall you know henceforth that whether you fight in Luther's cause or throw yourself at the feet of the Bishop of Rome, I shall never trust you more." The poor old man, thus harassed on all sides, found no longer any rest or comfort in his studies. Worn-out in body, and broken in spirit, he soon died.

The great source of Luther's hold on Germany lay in his direct appeal to the common people. For this he translated the Bible into German — even now the noblest version of the Bible in existence. For in translating a work of inspiration the intuition of a man like Luther, as Bayard Taylor has said, counts for more than the combined scholarship of a hundred men learned in the Greek and Hebrew. "The clear insight of one prophet is better than the average judgment of forty-seven scribes." The German language was then struggling into existence, and scholars considered it beneath their notice. It was fixed for all time by Luther's Bible. Luther often spent a week on a single verse to find and fix the idiomatic German. "It is easy to plow when the field is cleared," he said. "We must not ask the letters of the Latin alphabet how to speak German, but the mother in the kitchen and the plowman in the field, that they may know that the Bible is speaking German, and speaking to them. Out of the abundance of the heart the mouth speaketh. No German peasant would understand that. We must make it plain to him. '*Wess das Herz voll ist, dess geht der Mund über.*' ('Whose heart is full, his mouth runs over.')"

The same influence acted on Hutten. All his previous writings were in Latin, and were directed to scholars only. Henceforth he wrote the language of the Fatherland, and his appeals to the people were in language which the people could and did read. No Reformation ever came while only the learned and the noble were in the secret of it.

> "Latein, ich vor geschrieben hab
> Das war ein jeden nicht bekannt;
> Jetzt schrei ich an das Vaterland,
> Teutsch Nation in ihrer Sprach
> Zu bringen diesen Dingen Rach."

> ("For Latin wrote I hitherto,
> Which common people did not know.
> Now cry I to the Fatherland,

> The German people, in their tongue,
> Redress to bring for all these wrongs.")

A song for the people he now wrote, the "New
Song of Ulrich von Hutten," a song which stands
with Luther's "Ein feste Burg" in the history of
the Reformation:

> "Ich hab's gewagt mit Sinnen,
>   Und trag des noch kein Reu,
> Mag ich nit dran gewinnen,
>   Noch muss man spüren Treu.
>
> "Darmit ich mein
>   Mit eim allein,
> Wenn Man es wolt erkennen
>   Dem Land zu gut
>   Wiewol man thut
> Ein Pfaffenfeind mich nennen."

Part of this may be freely translated —

> "With open eyes I have dared it;
>   And cherish no regret,
> And though I fail to conquer,
>   The Truth is with me yet."

Hutten's dream in these days was of a league of
nobles, cities, and people, aided by the Emperor
if possible, against the Emperor if necessary, which
should by force of arms forever free Germany from
the rule of the Pope. Luther had little faith in the
power of force. "What Hutten wishes," he wrote

to a friend, "you see. But I do not wish to strive for the Gospel with murder and violence. Through the power of the Word is the world subdued; through the Word the Church shall be preserved and freed. Even Antichrist shall be destroyed by the power of the Word."

Now came the Great Diet at Worms, whither Luther was called before the Emperor to answer for his heretical teachings, and before which he stood firm and undaunted, a noble figure which has been a turning-point in history. "Here I stand. I can do nothing else. God help me."

Hutten, on his sick-bed at Ebernburg, not far away, was full of wrath at the trial of Luther. "Away!" he shouted, "away from the clear fountains, ye filthy swine! Out of the sanctuary, ye accursed peddlers! Touch no longer the altar with your desecrating hands. What have ye to do with the alms of our fathers, which were given for the poor and the Church, and you spend for splendor, pomp, and foolery, while the children suffer for bread? See you not that the wind of Freedom* is blowing? On two men not much depends. Know that there are many Luthers, many Huttens here. Should either of us be destroyed, still greater is

---

* "Sehet ihr nicht dasz die Luft der Freiheit weht?"

the danger that awaits you; for then, with those battling for freedom, the avengers of innocence will make common cause."

I have wished, in writing this little sketch, that I could have a novelist's privilege of bringing out my hero happily at the end. I have hitherto had the struggles of a man living before his time to relate; the voice of one crying in the wilderness. If this were a romance, I might tell how, with Hutten's entreaties and Luther's exhortations, and under the wise management of Franz von Sickingen, the people banded together against foreign foes and foreign domination, and German unity, German freedom, and religious liberty were forever established in the Fatherland. But, alas! the history does not run in that way; at least not till a hundred years of war had bathed the land in blood.

For Hutten henceforth I have only misery and failure to relate. The union of knights and cities resulted in a ruinous campaign of Franz von Sickingen against Trèves. Sickingen's army was driven back by the Elector. His strong Castle of Landstühl was besieged by the Catholic princes, and cannon was used in this siege for the first time in history. The walls of Landstühl, twenty-five feet thick, were battered down, and Sickingen himself was killed by the falling of a beam. The war was over, and nothing worthy had been accomplished.

When Luther heard of the death of Sickingen, he wrote to a friend: " Yesterday I heard and read of Franz von Sickingen's true and sad history. God is a righteous but marvelous Judge. Sickingen's fall seems to me a verdict of the Lord, that strengthens me in the belief that the force of arms is to be kept far from matters of the Gospel."

Hutten was driven from the Ebernburg. He was offered a high place in the service of the King of France; but, as a true German, he refused it, and fled, penniless and sick, to Basle, in Switzerland.

Here the great Humanist, Erasmus, reigned supreme. Erasmus disavowed all sympathy with his former friend and fellow-student. He called Hutten a dangerous and turbulent man, and warned the Swiss against him. Erasmus had noticed, with horror, in those who had studied Greek, that the influence of Lutheranism was fatal to learning; that zeal for philology decreased as zeal for religion increased. Already Erasmus, like Reuchlin, was ranged on the side of the Pope. So, in letters and pamphlets, Erasmus attacked Hutten; and the poet was not slow in giving as good as he received.

And this war between the Humanist and the Reformer gave great joy to the Obscurantists, who feared and hated them both.

"Humanism," says Strauss, "was broad-minded but faint-hearted, and in none is this better seen than in Erasmus. Luther was a narrower man, but his unvarying purpose, never looking to left nor right, was his strength. Humanism is the broad mirror-like Rhine at Bingen. It must grow narrower and wilder before it can break through the mountains to the sea."

Repulsed by Erasmus at Basle, Hutten fled to Mülhausen. Attacked by assassins there, he left at midnight for Zürich, where he put himself under the protection of Ulrich Zwingli. In Zwingli, the purest, loftiest, and clearest of insight of all of the leaders of the Reformation, Hutten found a congenial spirit. His health was now utterly broken. To the famous Baths of Pfäffers he went, in hope of release from pain. But the modern bath-houses of Ragatz were not built in those days, and the daily descent by a rope from above into the dark and dismal chasm was too much for his feeble strength. Then Zwingli sent him to a kindly friend, the Pastor Hans Schnegg, who lived on the little Island of Ufnau, in the Lake of Zürich.

ULRICH ZWINGLI.

And here at Ufnau, worn out by his long, double conflict with the Pope and with disease, Ulrich von Hutten died in 1523, at the age of thirty-five. "He left behind him," wrote Zwingli, "nothing of worth. Books he had none; no money, and no property of any sort, except a pen."

What was the value of this short and troubled life? Three hundred years ago it was easy to answer with Erasmus and the rest—Nothing. Hutten had denounced the Pope, and the Pope had crushed him. He had stirred up noble men to battle for freedom, and they, too, had been destroyed. Franz von Sickingen was dead. The league of the cities and princes had faded away forever. Luther was hidden in the Wartburg, no one knew where, and scarcely a trace of the Reformation was left in Germany. Whatever Hutten had touched he had ruined. He had "dared it," and the force he had defied had crushed him in return.

But, looking back over these centuries, the life of Hutten rises into higher prominence. His writings were seed in good ground. At his death the Reformation seemed hopeless. **Six years** later, at the second Diet of Spires, half Germany signed the protest which made us Protestants. "It was Luther alone who said *no* at the Diet of Worms. It was princes and people, cities and churches, who said *no* at the Diet of Spires."

Hutten's dream of a United German people freed from the yoke of Rome was for three hundred years unrealized. For the Reformation sundered the German people and ruined the German Empire, and not till our day has German unity come to pass. But, as later reformers said, "It is better that Germany should be half German, than that it should be all Roman."

For the true meaning of this conflict does not lie in any question of church against church or creed against creed, nor that worship in cathedrals with altars and incense and rich ceremony should give way to the simpler forms of the Lutheran litany. The issue was that of the growth of man. The "right of private interpretation" is the recognition of personal individuality.

The death of Hutten was, after all, not untimely. He had done his work. His was the "voice of one crying in the wilderness." The head of John the Baptist lay on the charger before Jesus had fulfilled his mission. Arnold Winkelried, at Sempach, filled his body with Austrian spears before the Austrian phalanx was broken. John Brown fell at Harper's Ferry before a blow was struck against slavery. Ulrich von Hutten had set every man, woman, and child in Germany to thinking of his relations to the Lord and to the Pope. His mission was completed; and longer life for him, as Strauss has suggested, might have led to discord among the Reformers themselves.

For this lover of freedom was intolerant of intolerance. For fine points of doctrine he had only contempt. When the Lutherans began to treat as enemies all Reformers who did not with them subscribe to the Confession of Augsburg, Hutten's fiery pen would have repudiated this confession. For he fought for freedom of the spirit, not for the Lutheran confession.

Had he remained in Switzerland, he would have been still less in harmony with the prevailing conditions. Not long after, Zwingli was slain in the wretched battle of Kappel, and, after him, the Swiss Reformation passed under the control of John Calvin. There can be no doubt that the stern pietist of Geneva would have burned Ulrich von Hutten with as calm a conscience as he did Michael Servetus.

The idea of a united and uniform Church, whether Catholic, Lutheran, or Calvinist, had little attraction for Hutten. He was one of the first to realize that religion is individual, not collective. It is concerned with life, not with creeds or ceremonies. In the high sense, no man can follow or share the religion of another. His religion, whatever it may be, is his own. It is built up from his own thoughts and prayers and actions. It is the expression of his own ideals. Only forms can be transferred unchanged from man to man, from generation to generation; never realities. For whatever is real to a man becomes part of him and partakes of his growth, and is modified by his personality.

Hutten was buried where he died, on the little island of Ufnau, in the Lake of Zürich, at the foot of the mighty Alps. And some of his old associates put over his grave a commemorative stone. Afterwards, the monks of the abbey of Einsiedeln, in Schwytz came to the island and removed the stone, and obliterated all traces of the grave.

It was well that they did so; for now the whole green island of Ufnau is his alone, and it is his worthy sepulcher.

NATURE–STUDY AND MORAL CULTURE.*

IN pleading for nature-study as a means of moral culture, I do not wish to make an overstatement, nor to claim for such study any occult or exclusive power. It is not for us to say, so much nature in the schools, so much virtue in the scholars. The character of the teacher is a factor which must always be counted in. But the best teacher is the one that comes nearest to nature, the one who is most effective in developing individual wisdom.

To seek knowledge is better than to have knowledge. Precepts of virtue are useless unless they are built into life. At birth, or before, "the gate of gifts is closed." It is the art of life, out of variant and contradictory materials passed down to us from our ancestors, to build up a coherent and effective individual character.

The essence of character-building lies in action. The chief value of nature-study in character-build-

---

* Read before the National Educational Association at Buffalo, New York, 1896.

ing is that, like life itself, it deals with realities. The experience of living is of itself a form of nature-study. One must in life make his own observations, frame his own inductions, and apply them in action as he goes along. The habit of finding out the best thing to do next, and then doing it, is the basis of character. A strong character is built up by doing, not by imitation, nor by feeling, nor by suggestion. Nature-study, if it be genuine, is essentially doing. This is the basis of its effectiveness as a moral agent. To deal with truth is necessary, if we are to know truth when we see it in action. To know truth precedes all sound morality. There is a great impulse to virtue in knowing something well. To know it well is to come into direct contact with its facts or laws, to feel that its qualities and forces are inevitable. To do this is the essence of nature-study in all its forms.

The claim has been made that history treats of the actions of men, and that it therefore gives the student the basis of right conduct. But neither of these propositions is true. History treats of the records of the acts of men and nations. But it does not involve the action of the student himself. The men and women who act in history are not the boys and girls we are training. Their lives are

developed through their own efforts, not by con-
templation of the efforts of others. They work out
their problem of action more surely by dissecting
frogs or hatching butterflies than by what we tell
them of Lycurgus or Joan of Arc. Their reason
for virtuous action must lie in their own knowledge
of what is right, not in the fact that Lincoln, or
Washington, or William Tell, or some other half-
mythical personage would have done so and so
under like conditions.

The rocks and shells, the frogs and lilies always
tell the absolute truth. Association with these, under right direction, will build up a habit of truthfulness, which the lying story of the cherry-tree
is powerless to effect. If history is to be made an
agency for moral training, it must become a nature-
study. It must be the study of original documents.
When it is pursued in this way it has the value of
other nature-studies. But it is carried on under
great limitations. Its manuscripts are scarce, while
every leaf on the tree is an original document in
botany. When a thousand are used, or used up, the
archives of nature are just as full as ever.

From the intimate affinity with the problems
of life, the problems of nature-study derive a large
part of their value. Because life deals with reali-

ties, the visible agents of the overmastering fates, it is well that our children should study the real, rather than the conventional. Let them come in contact with the inevitable, instead of the "made-up," with laws and forces which can be traced in objects and forms actually before them, rather than with those which seem arbitrary or which remain inscrutable. To use concrete illustrations, there is a greater moral value in the study of magnets than in the distinction between *shall* and *will*, in the study of birds or rocks than in that of diacritical marks or postage-stamps, in the development of a frog than in the longer or the shorter catechism, in the study of things than in the study of abstractions. There is doubtless a law underlying abstractions and conventionalities, a law of catechisms, or postage-stamps, or grammatical solecisms, but it does not appear to the student. Its consideration does not strengthen his impression of inevitable truth. There is the greatest moral value, as well as intellectual value, in the independence that comes from knowing, and knowing that one knows and why he knows. This gives spinal column to character, which is not found in the flabby goodness of imitation or the hysteric virtue of suggestion. Knowing what is right, and why it is right, before doing it is the basis of greatness of character.

The nervous system of the animal or the man is essentially a device to make action effective and to keep it safe. The animal is a machine in action. Toward the end of motion all other mental processes tend. All functions of the brain, all forms of nerve impulse are modifications of the simple reflex action, the automatic transfer of sensations derived from external objects into movements of the body.

The sensory nerves furnish the animal or man all knowledge of the external world. The brain, sitting in absolute darkness, judges these sensations, and sends out corresponding impulses to action. The sensory nerves are the brain's sole teachers; the motor nerves, and through them the muscles, are the brain's only servants. The untrained brain learns its lessons poorly, and its commands are vacillating and ineffective. In like manner, the brain which has been misued, shows its defects in ill-chosen actions — the actions against which Nature protests through her scourge of misery. In this fact, that nerve alteration means ineffective action, lying brain, and lying nerves, rests the great argument for temperance, the great argu-

ment against all forms of nerve tampering, from
the coffee habit to the cataleptic "revival of religion."

The senses are intensely practical in their relation
to life. The processes of natural selection make
and keep them so. Only those phases of reality
which our ancestors could render into action are
shown to us by our senses. If we can do nothing
in any case, we know nothing about it. The senses
tell us essential truth about rocks and trees, food
and shelter, friends and enemies. They answer no
problems in chemistry. They tell us nothing about
atom or molecule. They give us no ultimate facts.
Whatever is so small that we cannot handle it is
too small to be seen. Whatever is too distant to be
reached is not truthfully reported. The "X-rays"
of light we cannot see, because our ancestors could
not deal with them. The sun and stars, the clouds
and the sky are not at all what they appear to be.
The truthfulness of the senses fails as the square of
the distance increases. Were it not so, we should be
smothered by truth; we should be overwhelmed by
the multiplicity of our own sensations, and truthful response in action would become impossible.
Hyperæsthesia of any or all of the senses is a source
of confusion, not of strength. It is essentially a

phase of disease, and it shows itself in ineffectiveness, not in increased power.

Besides the actual sensations, the so-called realities, the brain retains also the sensations which have been, and which are not wholly lost. Memory-pictures crowd the mind, mingling with pictures which are brought in afresh by the senses. The force of suggestion causes the mental states or conditions of one person to repeat themselves in another. Abnormal conditions of the brain itself furnish another series of feelings with which the brain must deal. Moreover, the brain is charged with impulses to action passed on from generation to generation, surviving because they are useful. With all these arises the necessity for choice as a function of the mind. The mind must neglect or suppress all sensations which it cannot weave into action. The dog sees nothing that does not belong to its little world. The man in search of mushrooms "tramples down oak-trees in his walks." To select the sensations that concern us is the basis of the power of attention. The suppression of undesired actions is a function of the will. To find data for choice among the possible motor responses is a function of the intellect. Intellectual persistency is the essence of individual character.

As the conditions of life become more complex, it becomes necessary for action to be more carefully selected. Wisdom is the parent of virtue. Knowing what should be done logically precedes doing it. Good impulses and good intentions do not make action right or safe. In the long run, action is tested not by its motives, but by its results.

The child, when he comes into the world, has everything to learn. His nervous system is charged with tendencies to reaction and impulses to motion, which have their origin in survivals from ancestral experience. Exact knowledge, by which his own actions can be made exact, must come through his own experience. The experience of others must be expressed in terms of his own before it becomes wisdom. Wisdom, as I have elsewhere said, is knowing what it is best to do next. Virtue is doing it. Doing right becomes habit, if it is pursued long enough. It becomes a "second nature," or, we may say, a higher heredity. The formation of a higher heredity of wisdom and virtue, of knowing right and doing right, is the basis of character-building.

The moral character is based on knowing the best, choosing the best, and doing the best. It cannot be built up on imitation. By imitation, suggestion, and conventionality the masses are formed and controlled. To build up a man is a nobler process, demanding materials and methods of a higher order. The growth of man is the assertion of individuality. Only robust men can make history. Others may adorn it, disfigure it, or vulgarize it.

The first relation of the child to external things is expressed in this: What can I do with it? What is its relation to me? The sensation goes over into thought, the thought into action. Thus the impression of the object is built into the little universe of his mind. The object and the action it implies are closely associated. As more objects are apprehended, more complex relations arise, but the primal condition remains—What can I do with it? Sensation, thought, action—this is the natural sequence of each completed mental process. As volition passes over into action, so does science into art, knowledge into power, wisdom into virtue.

By the study of realities wisdom is built up. In the relations of objects he can touch and move, the child comes to find the limitations of his powers, the laws that govern phenomena, and to which his actions must be in obedience. So long as he deals with realities, these laws stand in their proper relation. "So simple, so natural, so true," says Agassiz.

"This is the charm of dealing with Nature herself. She brings us back to absolute truth so often as we wander."

So long as a child is lead from one reality to another, never lost in words or in abstractions, so long this natural relation remains. What can I do with it? is the beginning of wisdom. What is it to me? is the basis of personal virtue.

While a child remains about the home of his boyhood, he knows which way is north and which is east. He does not need to orientate himself, because in his short trips he never loses his sense of space direction. But let him take a rapid journey in the cars or in the night, and he may find himself in strange relations. The sun no longer rises in the east, the sense of reality in directions is gone, and it is a painful effort for him to join the new impressions to the old. The process of orientation is a difficult one, and if facing the sunrise in the morning were a deed of necessity in his religion, this deed would not be accurately performed.

This homely illustration applies to the child. He is taken from his little world of realities, a world in which the sun rises in the east, the dogs bark, the grasshopper leaps, the water falls, and the relation of cause and effect appear plain and natural.

In these simple relations moral laws become evident. "The burnt child dreads the fire," and this dread shows itself in action. The child learns what to do next, and to some extent does it. By practice in personal responsibility in little things, he can be led to wisdom in large ones. For the power to do great things in the moral world comes from doing the right in small things. It is not often that a man who knows that there is a right does the wrong. Men who do wrong are either ignorant that there is a right, or else they have failed in their orientation and look upon right as wrong. It is the clinching of good purposes with good actions that makes the man. This is the higher heredity that is not the gift of father or mother, but is the man's own work on himself.

The impression of realities is the basis of sound morals as well as of sound judgment. By adding near things to near, the child grows in knowledge. "Knowledge set in order" is science. Nature-study is the beginning of science. It is the science of the child. To the child training in methods of acquiring knowledge is more valuable than knowledge itself. In general, throughout life sound methods are more valuable than sound information. Self-direction is more important than innocence. The fool may be innocent. Only the sane and wise can be virtuous.

It is the function of science to find out the real nature of the universe. Its purpose is to eliminate the personal equation and the human equation in statements of truth. By methods of precision of thought and instruments of precision in observation, it seeks to make our knowledge of the small, the distant, the invisible, the mysterious as accurate as our knowledge of the common things men have handled for ages. It seeks to make our knowledge of common things exact and precise, that exactness and precision may be translated into action. The ultimate end of science, as well as its initial impulse, is the regulation of human conduct. To make right action possible and prevalent is the function of science. The "world as it is" is the province of science. In proportion as our actions conform to the conditions of the world as it is, do we find the world beautiful, glorious, divine. The truth of the "world as it is" must be the ultimate inspiration of art, poetry, and religion. The world as men have agreed to say it is, is quite another matter. The less our children hear of this, the less they will have to unlearn in their future development.

When a child is taken from nature to the schools, he is usually brought into an atmosphere of conventionality. Here he is not to do, but to imitate; not to see, nor to handle, nor to create, but to remember. He is, moreover, to remember not his own realities, but the written or spoken ideas of others. He is dragged through a wilderness of grammar, with thickets of diacritical marks, into the desert of metaphysics. He is taught to do right, not because right action is in the nature of things, the nature of himself and the things about him, but because he will be punished somehow if he does not.

He is given a medley of words without ideas. He is taught declensions and conjugations without number in his own and other tongues. He learns things easily by rote; so his teachers fill him with rote-learning. Hence, grammar and language have become stereotyped as teaching without a thought as to whether undigested words may be intellectual poison. And as the good heart depends on the good brain, undigested ideas become moral poison as well. No one can tell how much of the bad morals and worse manners of the conventional college boy of the past has been due to intellectual dyspepsia from undigested words.

In such manner the child is bound to lose his

orientation as to the forces which surround him. If he does not recover it, he will spend his life in a world of unused fancies and realities. Nonsense will seem half truth, and his appreciation of truth will be vitiated by lack of clearness of definition — by its close relation to nonsense.

That this is no slight defect can be shown in every community. There is no intellectual craze so absurd as not to have a following among educated men and women. There is no scheme for the renovation of the social order so silly that educated men will not invest their money in it. There is no medical fraud so shameless that educated men will not give it their certificate. There is no nonsense so unscientific that men called educated will not accept it as science.

It should be a function of the schools to build up common sense. Folly should be crowded out of the schools. We have furnished costly lunatic asylums for its accommodation. That our schools are in a degree responsible for current follies, there can be no doubt. We have many teachers who have never seen a truth in their lives. There are many who have never felt the impact of an idea. There are many who have lost their own orientation in their youth, and who have never since been able to point out the sunrise to others. It is no extravagance of language to say that diacritical marks lead to the cocaine habit; nor that the ethics of metaphysics points the way to the Higher Foolishness. There are many links in the chain of decadence, but its finger-posts all point downward.

"Three roots bear up Dominion—Knowledge, Will, the third, Obedience." This statement, which Lowell applies to nations, belongs to the individual man as well. It is written in the structure of his brain—knowledge, volition, action,—and all three elements must be sound, if action is to be safe or effective.

But obedience must be active, not passive. The obedience of the lower animals is automatic, and therefore in its limits measurably perfect. Lack of obedience means the extinction of the race. Only the obedient survive, and hence comes about obedience to "sealed orders," obedience by reflex action, in which the will takes little part.

In the early stages of human development, the instincts of obedience were dominant. Great among these is the instinct of conventionality, by which each man follows the path others have found safe. The Church and the State, organizations of the strong, have assumed the direction of the weak. It has often resulted that the wiser this direction, the greater the weakness it was called on to control. The "sealed orders" of human institutions took the place of the automatism of instinct. Against "sealed orders" the individual man has been in constant protest. The "warfare of science" was part of this long struggle. The Reformation, the revival of learning, the growth of democracy, are all phases of this great conflict.

The function of democracy is not good government. If that were all, it would not deserve the efforts spent on it. Better government than any king or congress or democracy has yet given could be had in simpler and cheaper ways. The automatic scheme of competitive examinations would give us better rulers at half the present cost. Even an ordinary intelligence office, or "statesman's employment bureau," would serve us better than conventions and elections. But a people which could be ruled in that way, content to be governed well by forces outside itself, would not be worth the saving. But this is not the point at issue. Government too good, as well as too bad, may have a baneful influence on men. Its character is a secondary matter. The purpose of self-government is to intensify individual responsibility; to promote abortive attempts

at wisdom, through which true wisdom may come
at last. Democracy is nature-study on a grand
scale. The republic is a huge laboratory of civics,
a laboratory in which strange experiments are
performed; but by which, as in other laboratories,
wisdom may arise from experience, and having
arisen, may work itself out into virtue.

"The oldest and best-endowed university in the
world," Dr. Parkhurst tells us, "is Life itself. Problems tumble easily apart in the field that refuse to
give up their secret in the study, or even in the
closet. Reality is what educates us, and reality
never comes so close to us, with all its powers of
discipline, as when we encounter it in action. In
books we find Truth in black and white; but in the
rush of events we see Truth at work. It is only
when Truth is busy and we are ourselves mixed up
in its activities that we learn to know of how much
we are capable, or even the power by which these
capabilities can be made over into effect."

Mr. Wilbur F. Jackman has well said: "Children
always start with imitation, and very few people
ever get beyond it. The true moral act, however,
is one performed in accordance with a known law
that is just as natural as the law which determines
which way a stone shall fall. The individual be-

comes moral in the highest sense when he chooses
to obey this law by acting in accordance with it."
Conventionality is not morality, and may co-exist
with vice as well as with virtue. Obedience has
little permanence unless it be intelligent obedience.

It is, of course, true that wrong information may
lead sometimes to right action, as falsehood may
secure obedience to a natural law which would
otherwise have been violated. But in the long run
men and nations pay dearly for every illusion they
cherish. For every sick man healed at Denver or
Lourdes, ten well men may be made sick. Faith
cure and patent medicines feed on the same vic-
tim. For every Schlatter who is worshiped as a
saint, some equally harmless lunatic will be stoned
as a witch. This scientific age is beset by the non-
science which its altruism has made safe. The
development of the common sense of the people
has given security to a vast horde of follies, which
would be destroyed in the unchecked competition
of life. It is the soundness of our age which has
made what we call its decadence possible. It is the
undercurrent of science which has given security
to human life, a security which obtains for fools as
well as for sages.

For protection against all these follies which so

soon fall into vices, or decay into insanity, we must look to the schools. A sound recognition of cause and effect in human affairs is our best safeguard. The old common sense of the "un-high-schooled man," aided by instruments of precision, and directed by logic, must be carried over into the schools. Clear thinking and clean acting, we believe, are results of the study of nature. When men have made themselves wise, in the wisdom which may be completed in action, they have never failed to make themselves good. When men have become wise with the lore of others, the learning which ends in self, and does not spend itself in action, they have been neither virtuous nor happy. "Much learning is a weariness of the flesh." Thought without action ends in intense fatigue of soul, the disgust with all the "sorry scheme of things entire," which is the mark of the unwholesome and insane philosophy of Pessimism. This philosophy finds its condemnation in the fact that it has never yet been translated into pure and helpful life.

With our children, the study of words and abstractions alone may, in its degree, produce the same results. Nature-studies have long been valued as a "means of grace," because they arouse the enthusiasm, the love of work which belongs to open-eyed youth. The child *blasé* with moral precepts and irregular conjugations turns with delight to the unrolling of ferns and the song of birds. There is a moral training in clearness and tangibility. An occult impulse to vice is hidden in all vagueness and in all teachings meant to be heard but not to be understood. Nature is never obscure, never occult, never esoteric. She must be questioned in earnest, else she will not reply. But to every serious question she returns a serious answer. "Simple, natural, and true" should make the impression of simplicity and truth. Truth and virtue are but opposite sides of the same shield. As leaves pass over into flowers, and flowers into fruit, so are wisdom, virtue, and happiness inseparably related.

THE HIGHER SACRIFICE.

THE HIGHER SACRIFICE.*

EACH man that lives is, in part, a slave, because he is a living being. This belongs to the definition of life itself. Each creature must bend its back to the lash of its environment. We imagine life without conditions—life free from the pressure of insensate things outside us or within. But such life is the dream of the philosopher. We have never known it. The records of the life we know are full of concessions to such pressure.

The vegetative part of life, that part which finds its expression in physical growth, and sustenance, and death, must always be slavery. The old primal hunger of the protoplasm rules over it all. Each of the myriad cells of which man is made must be fed and cared for. The perennial hunger of these cells he must stifle. This hunger began when life began. It will cease only when life ceases. It will last till the water of the sea is drained, the great lights are put out, and the useless earth is hung up empty in the archives of the universe.

---

*Address to the Graduating Class, Leland Stanford Jr. University, May 21, 1896.

This old hunger the individual man must each day meet and satisfy. He must do this for himself; else, in the long run, it will not be done. If others help feed him, he must feed others in return. This return is not charity nor sacrifice; it is simply exchange of work. It is the division of labor in servitude. Directly or indirectly, each must pay his debt of life. There are a few, as the world goes, who in luxury or pauperism have this debt paid for them by others. But there are not many of these fugitive slaves. The number will never be great; for the lineage of idleness is never long nor strong.

When this debt is paid, the slave becomes the man. Nature counts as men only those who are free. Freedom springs from within. No outside power can give it. Board and lodging on the earth once paid, a man's resources are his own. These he can give or hold. By the fullness of these is he measured. All acquisitions of man, Emerson tells us, "are victories of the good brain and brave heart; the world belongs to the energetic, belongs to the wise. It is in vain to make a paradise but for good men."

In the ancient lore of the Jews, so Rabbi Voorsanger tells us, it is written, "Serve the Lord, not as slaves hoping for reward, but as gods who will take no reward." The meaning of the old saying is this : *Only the gods can serve.*

Those who have nothing have nothing to give. He who serves as a slave serves himself only. That he hopes for a reward shows that to himself his service is really given. To serve the Lord, according to another old saying, is to help one's fellow-men. The Eternal asks not of mortals that they assist Him with His earth. The tough old world has been His for centuries of centuries before it came to be ours, and we can neither make it nor mar it. We were not consulted when its foundations were laid in the deep. The waves and the storms, the sunshine and the song of birds need not our aid. They will take care of themselves. Life is the only material that is plastic in our hand. Only man can be helped by man.

When they hung John Brown in Virginia, many said, you remember, that in resisting the Government he had thrown away his life, and would gain nothing for it. He could not, as Thoreau said at the time, get a vote of thanks or a pair of boots for his life. He could not get four-and-sixpence a day for being hung, take the year around. But he was not asking for a vote of thanks. It was not for the four-and-sixpence a day that he stood between brute force and its victims. It was to show men the nature of slavery. It was to help his fellow-citizens to read the story of their institutions in the light of history. " You can get more," Thoreau went on to say, " in your market [at Concord] for a quart of milk than you can for a quart of blood; but yours is not the market heroes carry their blood to." The blood of heroes is not sold by the quart. The great, strong, noble, and pure of this world, those who have made our race worthy to be called men, have not been paid by the day or by the quart; not by riches, nor fame, nor power, nor anything that man can give. Out of the fullness of their lives have they served the Lord. Out of the wealth of their resources have they helped their fellow-men.

The great man cannot be a self-seeker. The greatness of a Napoleon or an Alexander is the greatness of gluttony. It is slavery on a grand scale. What men have done for their own glory or aggrandizement has left no permanent impress. "I have carried out nothing," says the warrior, Sigurd Slembe. "I have not sown the least grain nor laid one stone upon another to witness that I have lived." Napoleon could have said as much, if, like Sigurd, he had stood "upon his own grave and heard the great bell ring." The tragedy of the Isle of St. Helena lay not in the failure of effort, but in the futility of the aim to which effort was directed. There was no tragedy of the Isle of Patmos.

What such men have torn down remains torn down. All this would soon have fallen of itself; for that which has life in it cannot be destroyed by force. But what such men have built has fallen when their hands have ceased to hold it up. The names history cherishes are those of men of another type. Only "a man too simply great to scheme for his proper self" is great enough to become a pillar of the ages.

It is part of the duty of higher education to build up ideals of noble freedom. It is not for help in the vegetative work of life that you go to college. You are just as good a slave without it. You can earn your board and lodging without the formality of culture. The training of the college will make your power for action greater, no doubt; but it will also magnify your needs. The debt of life a scholar has to pay is greater than that paid by the clown. And the higher sacrifice the scholar may be called upon to make grows with the increased fullness of his life. Greater needs go with greater power, and both mean greater opportunity for sacrifice.

In the days you have been with us you should have formed some ideals. You should have bound these ideals together with the chain of "well-spent yesterdays," the higher heredity which comes not from your ancestors, but which each man must build up for himself. You should have done something in the direction of the life of higher sacrifice, the life that from the fullness of its resources can have something to give.

Such sacrifice is not waste, but service; not spending, but accomplishing. Many men, and more women, spend their lives for others when others would have been better served if they had saved themselves. Mere giving is not service. "Charity that is irrational and impulsive giving, is a waste, whether of money or of life." "Charity creates half the misery she relieves; she cannot relieve half the misery she creates."

The men you meet as you leave these halls will not understand your ideals. They will not know that your life is not bound up in the present, but has something to ask or to give for the future. Till they understand you they will not yield you their sympathies. They may jeer at you because the whip they respond to leaves no mark upon you. They will try to buy you, because the Devil has always bid high for the lives of young men with ideals. A man in his market stands always above par. Slaves are his stock in trade. If a man of power can be had for base purposes, he can be sure of an immediate reward. You can sell your blood for its weight in milk, or for its weight in gold— whatever you choose,—if you are willing to put it up for sale. You can sell your will for the kingdoms of the earth; and you will see, or seem to see, many of your associates making just such bargains. But in this be not deceived. No young man worthy of anything else ever sold himself to the Devil. These are dummy sales. The Devil puts his own up at auction in hope of catching others. If you fall into his hands, you had not far to fall. You were already ripe for his clutches.

When a man steps forth from the college, he is tested once for all. It takes but a year or two to prove his mettle. In the college high ideals prevail, and the intellectual life is taken as a matter of course. In the world outside it appears otherwise, though the conditions of success are in fact just the same. It is not true, though it seems so, that the common life is a game of "grasping and

griping, with a whine for mercy at the end of it."
It is your own fault if you find it so. It is not
true that the whole of man is occupied with the
effort "to live just asking but to live, to live just
begging but to be." The world of thought and the
world of action are one in nature. In both truth
and love are strength, and folly and selfishness
are weakness. There is no confusion of right and
wrong in the mind of the Fates. It is only in our
poor bewildered slave intellects that evil passes for
power. All about us in the press of life are real
men, "whose fame is not bought nor sold at the
stroke of a politician's pen." Such are the men in
whose guidance the currents of history flow.

The lesson of values in life it should be yours
to teach, because it should be yours to know and
to act. Men are better than they seem, and the
hidden virtues of life appear when men have
learned how to translate them into action. Men
grasp and hoard material things because in their
poverty of soul they know of nothing else to do.
It is lack of training and lack of imagination,
rather than total depravity, which gives our social
life its sordid aspect. When a plant has learned
the secret of flowers and fruit, it no longer goes
on adding meaningless leaf on leaf. And as

"flowers are only colored leaves, fruits only ripe ones," so are the virtues only perfected and ripened forms of those impulses which show themselves as vices.

It is your relation to the overflow of power that determines the manner of man you are. Slave or god, it is for you to choose. Slave or god, it is for you to will. It is for such choice that will is developed. Say what we may about the limitations of the life of man, they are largely self-limitations. Hemmed in is human life by the force of the Fates; but the will of man is one of the Fates, and can take its place by the side of the rest of them. The man who can will is a factor in the universe. Only the man who can will can serve the Lord at all, and by the same token, hoping for no reward.

Likewise is love a factor in the universe. Power is not strength of body or mind alone. One who is poor in all else, may be rich in sympathy and responsiveness. "They also serve who only stand and wait."

In a recent number of The Dial, Mr. W. P. Reeves tells us the tale, half-humorous, half-allegorical, of the decadence of a scholar. According to this story, one Thomson was a college graduate, full of high notions of the significance of life and the duties and privileges of the scholar. With these ideals he went to Germany, that he might strengthen them and use them for the benefit of his fellow-men. He spent some years in Germany, filling his mind with all that German philosophy could give. Then he came home, to turn his philosophy into action. To do this, he sought a college professorship.

This he found it was not easy to secure. Nobody cared for him or his message. The authority of " wise and sober Germany" was not recognized in the institutions of America, and he found that college professorships were no longer " plums to be picked" by whomsoever should ask for them. The reverence the German professor commands is unknown in America. In Germany, the authority of wise men is supreme. Their words, when they speak, are heard with reverence and attention. In America, wisdom is not wisdom till the common man has examined it and pronounced it to be such. The conclusions of the scholar are revised by the daily newspaper. The readers of these papers care little for messages from Utopia.

No college opened its doors to Thomson, and he saw with dismay that the life before him was one of discomfort and insignificance, his ideals having no exchangeable value in luxuries or comforts. Meanwhile, Thomson's early associates seemed to get on somehow. The world wanted their cheap achievements, though it did not care for him.

Among these associates was one Wilcox, who became a politician, and, though small in abilities and poor in virtues, his influence among men seemed to be unbounded. The young woman who had felt an interest in Thomson's development, and to whom he had read his rejected verses and his uncalled-for philosophy, had joined herself to the Philistines, and yielded to their influence. She had become Wilcox's wife. His friends regarded Thomson's failure as a joke. He must not take himself too seriously, they said. A man should be in touch with his times. "Even Philistia," one said, "has its æsthetic ritual and pageantry." A wise man will not despise this ritual, because Philistinism, after all, is the life of the world.

But Thomson held out. " I pledged my word in Germany," he said, " to teach nothing that I did not believe to be true. I must live up to this pledge." And so he sought for positions, and he failed to find them. Finally, he had a message from a friend that a professorship in a certain institution was vacant. This message said, "Cultivate Wilcox."

So, in despair, Thomson began to cultivate Wilcox.
He began to feel that Wilcox was a type of the
world, a bad world, for which he was not responsible. The world's servant he must be, if he received
its wages. When he secured the coveted appoint-
ment, through the political pull of Wilcox and the
mild kindness of Mrs. Wilcox, he was ready to
teach whatever was wanted of him, whether it was
truth in Germany or not. He found that he could
change his notions of truth. The Wilcox idea was
that everything in America is all right just as it is.
To this he found it easy to respond. His salary
helped him to do so. And at last, the record says,
he became " *laudator temporis acti,*" one who praises
the times that are past. As such, he took but little
part in the times that are to be.

So runs the allegory. How shall it be with
you? There are many Thomsons among our
scholars. There may be some such among you.
When you pass from the world of thought you
will find yourself in the world of action. The
conditions are not changed, but they seem to be
changed. How shall you respond to the seeming difference? Shall you give up the truth of
high thinking for the appearance of speedy success? If you do this, it will not be because you

are worldly-wise, but because you do not know the world. In your ignorance of men you may sell yourself cheaply.

One must know life before he can know truth. He who will be a leader of men must first have the power to lead himself. The world is selfish and unsympathetic. But it is also sagacious. It rejects as worthless him who suffers decadence when he comes in contact with its vulgar cleverness. The natural man can look the world in the face. The true man will teach truth wherever he is,— not because he has pledged himself in Germany not to teach anything else, but because in teaching truth he is teaching himself. His life thus becomes genuine, and, sooner or later, the world will respond to genuineness in action. The world knows the value of genuineness, and it yields to that force wherever it is felt. "The world is all gates," says Emerson, "all opportunities, strings of tension waiting to be struck."

Thus, in the decadence of Thomson, it was not the times or the world or America that was at fault; it was Thomson himself. He had in him no life of his own. His character, like his microscope, "was made in Germany," and bore not his mark, but the stamp of the German factory. Truth was not made

in Germany; and to know or to teach truth there
must be a life behind it.   The decadence of Thomson was the appearance of the real Thomson from
under the axioms and formulæ his teachers had
given him.

Men do not fail because they are human.   They
are not human enough.   Failure comes from lack
of life.   Only the man who has formed opinions
of his own can have the courage of his convic-
tions.   Learning alone does not make a man strong.
Strength in life will show itself in helpfulness, will
show itself in sympathy, in sacrifice.   "Great men,"
says Emerson, "feel that they are so by renounc-
ing their selfishness and falling back on what is
humane.   They beat with the pulse and breathe
with the lungs of nations."

It is not enough to know truth; one must know
men.   It is not enough to know men; one must be
a man.   Only he who can live truth can know it.
Only he who can live truth can teach it.   "He
could talk men over," says Carlyle of Mirabeau,
"he could talk men over because he could act men
over.   At bottom that was it."

And at bottom this is the source of all power
and service.   Not what a man knows, or what he
can say; but what is he? what can he can do?

Not what he can do for his board and lodging, as the slave who is "hired for life"; but what can he do out of the fullness of his resources, the fullness of his helpfulness, the fullness of himself? The work the world will not let die was never paid for — not in fame, not in money, not in power.

The decadence of literature, of which much is said to-day, is not due to the decadence of man. It is not the effect of the nerve strain of over-wrought generations born too late in the dusk of the ages. Its nature is this—that uncritical and untrained men have come into a heritage they have not earned. They will pay money to have their feeble fancy tickled. The decadence of literature is the struggle of mountebanks to catch the public eye. There is money in the literature of decay, and those who work for money have "verily their reward." But these performances are not the work of men. They have no relation to literature, or art, or human life. These are not in decadence because imitations are sold on street-corners or tossed into our laps on railway trains. As well say that gold is in its decadence because brass can be burnished to look like it; or that the sun is in his dotage because we have filled our gardens with Chinese lanterns.

"No ray is dimmed, no atom worn,
    My oldest force is good as new
And the fresh rose on yonder thorn
    Gives back the bending heavens in dew."

Literature has never been paid for. It has never asked the gold nor the plaudits of the multitude. Job, and Hamlet, and Faust, and Lear, were never written to fill the pages of a Sunday newspaper. John Milton and John Bunyan were not publishers' hacks; nor were John Hampden, John Bright, or Samuel Adams under pay as walking-delegates of reform.

No man was hired to find out that the world was round, or that the valleys are worn down by water, or that the stars are suns. No man was paid to burn at the stake or die on the cross that other men might be free to live. The sane, strong, brave, heroic souls of all ages were the men who, in the natural order of things, have lived above all considerations of pay or glory. They have served not as slaves hoping for reward, but as gods who would take no reward. Men could not reward Shakespeare, or Darwin, or Newton, or Helmholtz for their services any more than we could pay the Lord for the use of His sunshine. From the same inexhaustible divine reservoir it all comes—the service of the great man and the sunshine of God.

"Twice have I molded an image,
    And thrice outstretched my hand;
Made one of day and one of night,
    And one of the salt sea strand ·
One in a Judean manger,
    And one by Avon's stream;
One over against the mouths of Nile,
    And one in the Academe."

And in such image are men made every day, not
only in Bethlehem or in Stratford, not alone on the
banks of the Nile or the Arno; but on the Columbia, or the Sacramento, or the San Francisquito, it
may be, as well. All over the earth, in this image,
are the sane, and the sound, and the true. And
when and where their lives are spent arises generations of others like them, men in the true order.
Not alone men in the "image of God," but "gods
in the likeness of men."

It is to the training of the genuine man that the
universities of the world are devoted. They call for
the higher sacrifice, the sacrifice of those who have
powers not needed in the common struggle of life,
and who have, therefore, something over and beyond this struggle to give to their fellows. Large
or small, whatever the gift may be, the world needs
it all, and to every good gift the world will respond
a thousand-fold. Strength begets strength, and
wisdom leads to wisdom. "There is always room

for the man of force, and he makes room for many."
It is the strong, wise, and good of the past who
have made our lives possible. It is the great human men, the "men in the natural order," that
have made it possible for "the plain, common
men," that make up civilization, to live, rather
than merely to vegetate.

We hear those among us sometimes who complain of the shortness of life, the smallness of truth,
the limited stage on which man is forced to act.
But the men who thus complain are not men who
have filled this little stage with their action. The
man who has learned to serve the Lord never com-
plains that his Master does not give him enough to
do. The man who helps his fellow-men does not
stand about with idle hands to find men worthy of
his assistance. He who leads a worthy life never
vexes himself with the question as to whether life
is worth living.

We know that all our powers are products of the
needs and duties of our ancestors. Wisdom too
great to be translated into action is an absurdity.
For wisdom is only knowing what it is best to do
next. Virtue is only doing it. Virtue and happiness have never been far apart from each other.
To know and to do is the essence of the highest

service.   Those the world has a right to honor are
those who found enough in the world to do.   The
fields are always white to their harvest.

Alexander the Great had conquered his neighbors in Greece and Asia Minor, the only world he
knew.   Then he sighed for more worlds to conquer.   But other worlds he knew nothing of lay
all about him.   The secrets of the rocks he had
never suspected.   Steam, electricity, the growth of
trees, the fall of snow,— all these were mysteries
to him.   The only conquest he knew, the subjec-
tion of men's bodies, went but a little way.   All
the men who in his lifetime knew the name of
Alexander the Great could find encampment on
the Palo Alto farm.   The great world of men in
his day was beyond his knowledge.   His world
was a very small one, and of this he had seen but
a little corner.

For the need of more worlds to conquer is no
badge of strength.   It is the stamp of ignorance.
It is the cry only of him who knows that the
great earth about him still stands unconquered.
No Lincoln ever sighed for more nations to save;
no Luther for more churches to purify; no Darwin that nature had not more hidden secrets which
he might follow to their depths; no Agassiz that

the thoughts of God were all exhausted before he was born.

And now, a final word to you as scholars: Higher education means the higher sacrifice. That you are taught to know is simply that you may do. Knowing the truth signifies that you should do right. Knowing and doing have value only as translated into justice and love. There is no man so strong as not to need your help. There is no man so weak that you cannot make him stronger. There is none so sick that you cannot bring him to the "gate called Beautiful." There is no evil in the world that you cannot help turn to goodness. "We could lift up this land," said Björnson of Norway, "we could lift up this land, if we lifted as one."

Therefore lift, and lift as one. You are strong enough and wise enough. You shall seek strength and wisdom, that others through you may be wiser and stronger. You shall seek your place to work as your basis for helpfulness. Others will make the place as good as you deserve. If your lives are sacrificed in helping men, it is to the market of the ages you carry your blood, not to the milk-market of Concord town. The honest man will not "pledge himself in Germany to teach nothing which is not true." Being true himself, he can teach nothing false. The more men of the true order there are in the world, the greater is the world's need of men.

As you are men, so will your places in life be secure. Every profession is calling you. Every walk of life is waiting for your effort. There will always be room for you, and each of you will make room for many.

THE BUBBLES OF SÁKI.

*I*N *sad, sweet cadence Persian Omar sings*
The life of man that lasts but for a day;
A phantom caravan that hastes away,
On to the chaos of insensate things.

" The Eternal Sáki from that bowl hath poured
Millions of bubbles like us and shall pour,"
Thy life or mine, a half-unspoken word,
A fleck of foam tossed on an unknown shore.

" When thou and I behind the veil are past,
Oh, but the long, long while the world shall last!
Which of our coming and departure heeds,
As the seven seas shall heed a pebble cast."

" Then, my beloved, fill the cup that clears
To-day of past regrets and future fears."
This is the only wisdom man can know,
" I come like water, and like wind I go."

But tell me, Omar, hast thou said the whole?
If such the bubbles that fill Sáki's bowl,

How great is Sáki, whose least whisper calls
Forth from the swirling mists a human soul!

Omar, one word of thine is but a breath,
A single cadence in thy perfect song;
And as its measures softly flow along,
A million cadences pass on to death.

Shall this one word withdraw itself in scorn,
Because 't is not thy first, nor last, nor all—
Because 't is not the sole breath thou hast drawn,
Nor yet the sweetest from thy lips let fall?

I do rejoice that when " of Me and Thee "
Men talk no longer, yet not less, but more,
The Eternal Sáki still that bowl shall fill,
And ever stronger, purer bubbles pour.

One little note in the Eternal Song,
The Perfect Singer hath made place for me;
And not one atom in earth's wondrous throng
But shall be needful to Infinity.